MW01041863

A Journey of Brothers

Novella I

Linda J. Pedley

A Journey of Brothers

ISBN#978-0-9878319-7-2

This book is dedicated to my mom

~ BJ ~

Thank you for supporting me as I traversed my own way so I might discover this wonderful world through my writing journey. Your encouragement and acceptance of my writing is something I will remember and treasure always. You loved this story and saw great things for it – I appreciate your review, input, and suggestions. It will be forever special to me knowing how much you liked it.

Miss you.

Love you always.

Table of Contents

Chapter 1 – Into the Forest

They were told the only way to make it safely through the forest to the next village was to stay off of the road. With their mother's whispered love and a repeated warning, they entered the forest where the undergrowth was the thickest.

"Be safe my babes and God speed." She waved as they both turned to smile, small unsure but brave smiles, just before the leaves and the brush swallowed them into the grove.

"Remember, stay off of the road." She called out to them again, but they were gone. Aaslan took his assigned duty seriously and vowed he would escort his younger sister, Aisha, safely to the walled centre of Balikesir, forty miles as the crow flies situated just beyond the dark forest of Belgrade. Even as a boy, he realized the danger of travel through the untamed territories, but under the cover of the forest, and in silence, they had a chance. Stories of the renegade Road Rogues filled his head with horrors as he recalled overhearing tales in the village market square. He was not afraid and his promise to his mother made him even more determined to deliver his charge safely to their uncle who awaited their arrival on the other side. With the lessons from her mother tucked solidly in her learning, Aisha would be a valuable help to their aunt who was expecting their first child. She was due the following week and it would take a couple of days travel; they would arrive with plenty of time before the baby arrived.

"Shhh, Aisha, we must be as silent as the deer in the night." Aaslan whispered his warning, leaning close to his sister's ear, as they continued their steady trek.

At fourteen, she was obedient and accepting to the ways of her world. She turned her face to him, nodded, and just smiled. From his pocket he took a handful of shelled chestnuts and offered a share to her. She nibbled happily on the treat and stepped cautiously over fallen limbs and outstretched roots. Their footsteps were quiet as they made their way through the brush, ducking easily under outstretched branches. New undergrowth cushioned the forest floor making late spring an ideal time for travel. New foliage rustled softly overhead. Fall would not have been a good time to be traipsing through the forest.

At the first creek that cut through the trees about two miles into their journey, they rested a moment, taking a refreshing mouthful of cool water. Aisha set her pack on the ground and stretched. A short whistle, like the sound of a small bird, broke the silence and Aisha looked up questioningly to her brother. He put a finger to his lips.

They waited, but no immediate sound followed. He cautioned her and she watched for his signal, remaining still. A few moments later, the sound broke the silence again with two short bursts this time.

"Aaslan, it is a bird."

She veered off suddenly to the left and he frantically grabbed for her arm. She was quick and bolted through the edge of the oak stand and into the high grass that lined the roadway just beyond the cover of the trees.

"What's this?"

Aisha almost ran headlong into the strong legs of a shaggy mount. She looked up at the man on the horse, her eyes wide, her mouth open but no sound escaped.

"Little rag, come here. You'll fetch a pretty penny at the trade."

He was off of his horse in a flash and scooped her up under his arm. Her scream found sound and it echoed on the silence of the air.

"Aaslan!"

Just then Aaslan burst from the trees and the man's horse startled. The now crying girl was wrapped and held tightly by another Rogue sitting high astride his dirty grey mount. The men wore hide capes that hung from leather straps at their shoulders; wide belts held two long-knives crisscrossed through the front. The first man grabbed one knife from its sheath and waved it in the boy's direction.

"And just what might you be, young lad?" He laughed a deep, throaty bellow as Aaslan stopped short in his tracks. "Come fight Sagiv and I'll stick you like a pig and leave you lying for the beasts of the night to feast on." This time both men laughed as they gathered their horses making ready to leave.

"No, please! Aisha!"

"Aaslan!"

Aisha's screams for him were the last thing he heard as the two men on horseback galloped off, leaving him standing in the underbrush. He ran after them, shouting and waving, until his legs and arms were tired even though he knew he did not have a chance to catch them on foot. He finally gave up and stood in the middle of the road watching helplessly as the dust settled in the distance. He bit his lip, fighting off the initial urge to cry – he promptly admonished himself as he had not the pleasure of being a young boy privy to giving in to defeat out here in the wilderness. There was no one else to depend on - he had been given a simple mission and already, so soon into the journey, he failed. Gathering his wisdom and wits about him, he returned to retrieve his pack. If he was going to go after his sister he needed supplies.

Aaslan continued along the open road longer than he knew he should, and as the waning sunlight cast shadows, he realized he must find a safe limb in a tree to spend the night. He would have to get some sleep –

for this day, in his darkest hour, his journey was clear. He would not leave his sister to the mercy of the Road Rogues. He would not stop his hunt until he found her and brought her home again.

Chapter 2 – The Hunter

The mist from the overnight rain rose from the sodden fields as the sun began its morning stretch over the eastern horizon. Aaslan shaded his eyes. Peering into the dewy veils, he half expected her to call out. He could not erase the screams of his name, the pleading helplessness in her voice that haunted him as he trudged wearily through the countryside.

After leaving the cover of protective forest, the warmth of the sun was soothing, comforting, but almost too pleasant a feeling for the turmoil he was experiencing inside. His gut rolled and churned; he was too focused on his tracking to realize it was probably just hunger that beckoned and not an unwanted malaise.

Several times, he set his pack down to inspect the tracks left by the horses; the trail grew colder as he followed slowly. And several times, he had to remind himself to take his belongings with him, so sharp was his focus on the grounded hoof prints. As long as he could see them, he knew he was at least going in the right direction. He also knew the Road Rogues would make their way to the less desirable districts of Istanbul to the slave market. He heard that the market was only open to trade in the late spring - he must hurry, as the changing of the seasons would soon be upon them and the market would move on. He must not lose his chance to save his sister.

A sudden noise from behind startled him out of his reverie and instinctively he started to run, the long grass whipping his legs, thick shrubbery scratching at his ankles. He came to an abrupt halt as a horse materialized in front of him. *I cannot outrun another mountain horse*, were his weary thoughts, as the man riding her cut off his escape route. Aaslan sank to the ground in a heap, his shoulders shook with heavy sobs.

"Please, mister, do not hurt me. I must find my sister." His voice was pleading and muffled as he spoke into his dirt covered hands.

"I mean you no harm." The voice was gruff but sincere.

Aaslan glanced cautiously up to the man who now stood beside him; his horse grazed contentedly a few feet away.

"Who are you, sir?" Aaslan was careful to be respectful. Even though he did not know the man, he sensed friendliness about him. No weapon was drawn or visible. *Perhaps*, he chanced the hope, *this man could help me.*

"I am called Udmurt."

"I have not heard of you. Where are you from?"

Aaslan noted the details of the man's clothes and boots, his horse and his trappings - nothing seemed familiar to him, but he realized, too, as still a boy he had not traveled far from home, until now.

"I am from the Ural Mountains in Russia, north of here. Now what might you be doing out here all alone?" The man moved to the pack slung over the horse's hind quarters and dug out a small leather wrap. From inside, he withdrew a piece of dried pastirma, and offered it to Aaslan. "Go, on. Take it. What is your name, boy?"

"I am Aaslan; son of Aydin. I am from the village Bursa, north of Balikesir. I cannot waste any more time talking - the Road Rogues took my sister and I must find her."

"Admirable," Udmurt mumbled in between bites of his seasoned beef.

"I am following their trail."

"And what do you propose to do once you find them?"

Udmurt let out a low chuckle. The sound, even if in jest, prodded Aaslan's ego as if he were skewered with a long blade.

"You do not have to come along. I did not ask for your help. It is my duty to find her for she was in my care when she was taken. It is my responsibility to find them and bring her home."

"No need to get all ruffled and besides who said I was going to come along?"

Aaslan could not help the tears that formed in his eyes. He tried to put on a brave front, but it was merely a show. The burden he carried showed in his face as a plea, yet defiant as a lion he would do what he had to do, without asking.

Udmurt gathered the reins and lifted himself easily into the saddle. He sat for a moment looking down on the boy. The horse shook its head impatiently. Udmurt patted the oil cloth pack behind him and extended a gloved hand.

"So which way did they go?"

Chapter 3 – Captive

Aisha's eyes remained closed long past the time she actually woke for fear of what she might see. The journey to this end was rough – her body ached from its three day ride strapped to the back of one of the Road Rogue's mountain ponies. Her wrists were now wrapped in a thin layer of gauze. Underneath, they were raw from the leather bindings that held her tight and in the spots where the flesh had been sliced through they only now stopped bleeding.

Her throat was dry and sore from the dust. She had only stopped screaming when the sounds of Aaslan's voice calling out to her faded into the distance. Soon, all she could hear was the pounding of the horse's hooves and when the drone became a part of her, she stopped trying to think. Her reality would now be for survival and, although she knew in her heart Aaslan would never abandon his search for her, she realized it was up to her to stay alive. The Turkish jewel was never a desired destination to her, but she surmised that the Middle Eastern Mecca would be a welcome change from the conditions she endured while in the hands of her captors.

The cot beneath her was rough and smelled of stale hay; she was thankful it was dry and supported by a sturdy frame that kept her up off the ground. Aisha slowly opened her eyes behind the protective shield of her hands. Through her fingers she could see the room was half lit with two lanterns mounted four feet apart along one of the whitewashed walls. She heard voices from the hall outside the darkened doorway and remained still, as if asleep.

A woman, she thought at first to be much older, came into the room with a jug. She sloshed some water into a small metal cup and extended it to Aisha.

"I know you don't sleep. Take this."

Aisha sat obediently and reached for the cup, nodding. She pushed herself back until she sat against the wall and pulled her loose knit sweater close to her body. She gobbled the cool liquid greedily, letting it slide over her tongue.

"You keep quiet and do as you are told." The woman grabbed the cup from Aisha's hands and their eyes met. The look was not menacing and it did not match the message she conveyed.

As Aisha continued to watch the woman, she realized she was probably not that many years older than herself, and wondered of her position. Her mind recalled the vivid tales told, of life outside her village home, shared by those who made the journey into the busy centres. She could not erase the pictures forged in her imagination. They were given to her as teachings and now were warnings her young years of fourteen did not reflect. She knew the knowledge and wisdom she possessed would help her survive. She would have to adapt quickly to handle the situation with maturity; though it had been some time since she succumbed to tears and turned to the solace of little girl comforts.

The girl blew out the flames that lit the dull room and threw Aisha a tattered shawl as she left.

"It gets cold in here despite the early season's daytime heat."

Again, Aisha could only nod her thanks and pulled the woven camel hair and wool wrap around her shoulders. Before the light faded into dusk, she memorized her surroundings. A small basin in the corner only steps from her cot; a high small barred window with heavy paper woven in and out to block the narrow view; mosquito netting draped through a metal ring protruding from the wall and wound around the frame of the bed; a path on the dirty floor worn on the stonework from the bed to the door.

As the last light of another day faded into night, Aisha pulled the netting down to surround her, tucking it in under the thin mattress. She lay down; the shawl pulled tight up over her shoulders to her neck and closed her eyes. She whispered a prayer while holding fast to her naïve young girl beliefs in the beauty of mankind.

In all that is glorious, oh beautiful Flora, you are my hope as sure as the flowers of spring after a deep winter's sleep. In my darkest moments, keep me safe and may the west wind Zephyr guide and protect my brother, Aaslan, until we are united again."

Her whisper became hushed as she heard the sound of footsteps stopping outside the locked door.

Chapter 4 – Prince Emir

It seemed like forever, but finally the footsteps moved on and the night became her solace. A tormented sleep tossed her about and many times during the night Aisha awoke to the sounds of a different place, disturbing and haunting, forever trying to pry another scream; she remained silent. It was the only way she knew she might preserve her strength and sustain her survival. Quiet as the night, she was determined to just exist, blending in, and perhaps, she would go unnoticed.

She did not presume she was the only one being held; the stories reminded her that success at the slave trade was based on numbers, and the more bodies a seller could present, the more gold he could collect in his pocket. There were no sounds in the night to lead Aisha to believe there were other women on the other sides of the walls that held her captive – a silence that was both disturbing and encouraging. A restless night finally grew into a welcome sleep as she became weary with worry and thought.

The sound of a key in the lock and voices outside the door startled Aisha awake. She was surprised to see a sliver of light now peeking its way in from the small window as the morning sun greeted her. She silently said a prayer of thanks to the night gods for watching over her while she slept.

The young woman, who brought her water the night before, entered through the door, her voice sharp as she replied in apparent answer to an unheard question from someone who stood just outside in the hallway. Aisha could not see who it was from her place in the middle of the bed.

"Come, girl."

The woman beckoned to her and pulled the mosquito netting away so Aisha could step out of the bed. She leaned in close to Aisha's ear while her hand held a firm grip on the girl's arm.

"Remember - stay quiet and do as you are told." Their eyes met, and for a moment, Aisha thought the girl would say more, but the feeling was fleeting and smothered as a blindfold was wrapped around Aisha's eyes.

"Please, no."

"Shhh. Quiet. Remember - do as you are told."

Aisha felt pain in her wrists as bindings were strapped to her and she fought to contain the overwhelming feeling of despair threatening inside. She mustered all the strength she could, and by using her other senses to guide her, she followed the lead of the girl as they left the small room. The stone floor felt cold on her feet and the lack of light or warmth of sun meant to Aisha they stayed inside, *perhaps in a tunnel or a passage way of some kind,* she surmised. There were no sounds, save for the fall of their footsteps and the heavy breathing of their guide. She could feel the girl's hand on her arm as she steered her along; uncertainty lived in that touch for she knew not the role of her caretaker. She could trust no one.

They paused for a moment and the opening of a large door groaned in the silence. From within, there came the sound of laughter and music; the heat of a hearth somewhere deep in the room emitted the aroma of burning wood and the sweet smell of a flower Aisha could not place. She knew there was light and warmth beyond her binds, but she was uncertain if that was a good place. Not all merriment could be considered safe.

The girl pulled the blindfold from Aisha's eyes and, with a whispered reminder to do as she was told, pushed her into the light and left the same way they entered. The guard who accompanied them closed the large wooden door and stood in front of it. The saber at his side was sheathed in a jewel encrusted case and his hand rested calmly, yet ready, upon the hilt.

She turned to face the room. Silk woven tapestries adorned every wall and there were rich velvet upholstered hassocks scattered throughout the lantern lit room. An alcove with thick cushions and draped curtains and sweet smelling candles was the center of attention. Girls with long shiny black hair, dressed in shimmering fabrics, moved about the room to the rhythm of the music. When the door closed with a thud, the dancing stopped and all attention turned to Aisha. Veils hid faces, but dark eyes warned her of her intrusion.

"Come. Come, girls. Is that any way to treat our guest?"

The voice came from the alcove amongst the satin cushions and soon a man, with the darkest eyes and hair Aisha had ever seen, pushed his way through the harem. His smile was directed to her and she watched as he approached, his hands extended. He looked her up and down, and Aisha stared down at the floor.

"No. No. My young beauty, look directly at me. Come – rest and I will get you something to eat and to drink. The girls will take care of you. Prince Emir will take care of you." He held her hand and led her to the alcove where the soft pillows beckoned and the whole world could be closed out with one tug on the braided cords.

The prince left the room, and for a moment, Aisha was panicked. Not sure what was to happen, she remembered the warnings and remained quiet while obeying what she was told. She sat on a hassock and, by the light of a candle, a young girl combed her hair while another washed her face. They tugged at her dirty linen dress and sheath, pulling it over her head. With all the girls flitting about, she had no time for modesty as they continued to wash her and then spritzed her with fragrant water. A freshly laundered white muslin gown soon covered her, its layers of brushed gauze soothing against her skin.

They motioned her to the center of the alcove and she reclined, feeling relaxed and, oddly, at home. As the girls left her, she saw him approach and with one pull of the cords, he draped them together into a single silent world. His princely smile mesmerized her. He slipped the cotton tunic off over his head and, for a brief moment, shadows quivered on the wall as the candle flickered, then fizzled to nothing.

Chapter 5 – Encounter on the Road

The day was long but their north eastern progress over a well trodden path marked by two heavy mountain ponies, kept the hope alive and the promise fresh in his heart. Aaslan knew he would have kept to the road even if his more than accommodating travel companion, Udmurt, had not by chance happened upon him. At some point, he would thank the man for his generosity in whatever manner he could, but until the time proved well and the task complete, he knew he needed the man as much as he tried to convince himself he could do the quest alone.

"I was going to take the other trail, west to the Mediterranean."

It was a statement that came out of the blue and Aaslan was unsure of its intent. It did not even sound like it was directed to him, but since he was the only one in earshot he would have to assume, it was because of him.

"I did not ask you to come." Aaslan's voice was muffled into the large man's back as they plodded along the track, almost eight hours and the better part of a day gone.

"I know, young lad, I was just saying – no mind, a full summer ahead allows me this slight diversion."

Aaslan did not have to raise his concern for their slow progress, for as if in silent answer, Udmurt urged his mount forward in a trot.

"We will make up some time before nightfall and then find a suitable camp. I think our calm weather is about to end."

The boy watched as a flock of ducks scuttled from the nearby marsh shore and settled deeper into the reeds and tall grass already growing thick and dense on the opposite side, sheltered by the wind row.

There was a cool breeze in the late afternoon air and a grey mist formed over the distant fields. He knew if he really concentrated on what was going on around him, he too, was aware of these things; his father had taught him from an early age how to read Mother Nature's signs. This attention to detail slipped his mind easily with a task so focused as the one he had become narrow-minded to - finding his sister. It was certain he would not succeed, however, if he did not survive. He brought his mind back to the road ahead and made a conscious effort to stay in the moment.

"How far to Istanbul?"

"Three days ride."

"Can we not make it sooner? I know the trade leaves the great city shortly after the solstice. I cannot let her be taken away." The distress in his voice betrayed his momentary resolve to encounter whatever obstacles he met, head on. He was struggling to prove his manhood in a boy's body while dealing with an unrelenting world.

"We will make it and you will find her." Udmurt's voice was low as he directed the comment over his shoulder to Aaslan. He held up a hand and Aaslan followed the gloved finger as it pointed to the horse's ears. "You must stay strong, remain alert, and focus on getting there first."

Without warning, he pulled the lead a sharp right and the big horse took surefooted steps into the long grass. As they came to the edge of the trees, Udmurt grabbed Aaslan's arm as he swung his leg over the horse's neck and together they slid to the soft ground. Hidden behind a thick bay tree, they were able to shield themselves and the horse from view of the path. Udmurt motioned for Aaslan to remain still and quiet while he covered a leather hand over the muzzle of his horse and put his forehead to her neck.

"Aaaah, sessiz, Hazine." The horse was quiet and relaxed under his master's touch and voice.

A few tense moments passed until the sound of heavy wooden wheels rumbled into earshot. Slow, plodding ponies signified a heavy laden cart and perhaps a full day's work soon to come to a close. As the procession filed by, within yards of their hiding spot, Aaslan held his breath. He wanted to peek through quivering fingers to see who might be approaching from the very direction they were headed. His thoughts were only on finding out news that might help his plight. He did not think for a moment they were in trouble of any kind even though his large companion hurried them from open view.

The footsteps and hoof falls and wagon, stopped.

Aaslan's held breath exhaled in what he thought was a thunderous roar and his face felt icy cold as the blood drained away in fear. Udmurt shielded Aaslan, and they waited. They could hear the wagon master's noisy descent, ending with a grunt as he landed hard on the packed clay. The sound of heavy boots trampling the long grasses came toward them and it would be only a few moments before their hiding place would be revealed.

Udmurt leapt from the thicket in silence and in stealth. There was a low groan and a rumble of foreign words that Aaslan could only imagine their meaning, as large solid bodies hit and fell to the ground with a clash of metal upon metal. He did not want to die there in a thicket of bay leaves along a road to Istanbul. He had imagined his end might come in a valiant attempt to free his sister from whatever malice might hold her, but not here, not yet. He was ill prepared to make so soon a stand yet grabbed a thick branch of deadfall and charged from the brush. The makeshift weapon raised, he rushed the dueling pair. Udmurt put up a hand to wield the blow upon his leather glove.

"Are you meaning to kill me with a twig, young master?"

There was a roar of laughter from the man lying on the ground, and Udmurt rolled over on his back, unable to contain an equally loud regale. When he was finally calm, he sat up and spoke quietly.

"Aaslan, brave son of Aydin, this is my friend, Izmir."

The man sat up, and still chuckling, managed a yellow toothy grin. He extended a leather wrapped hand in a gesture of good faith which Aaslan angrily ignored.

"I hate you both."

Aaslan threw the stick to the ground and disappeared into the trees; the leaves and twigs crunched beneath his feet, his destination unknown.

Chapter 6 –Prince Haidar

Filtered lights from outside the private alcove gave Prince Emir's skin a sultry glow as he threw the cotton tunic aside. His black hair hung just to his shoulder and he brushed it back from his forehead, as he watched her, watching him. Her little girl heart fluttered and she wondered on these new feelings, in fear but inquisitive, too. She remembered seeing her own brother in this stage of undress and did not recall this type of emotion set within her. It must be the feeling she knew her mother had for her father and she now understood. Her body felt like it was on fire as the panic set in, and she realized it was probably a fever from being ill-kept for so many days. Her stomach felt like it was still enslaved.

His hand slid over the hide covered cushions and up her foot to her ankle. She let out a scream that she stifled quickly with the long muslin sleeve on her loose fitting dress. She pulled both her feet up under her as she scrambled to put as much distance between them as she could. The wall at her back limited her escape.

"Do not be afraid, young one, I will not harm you."

His voice was soothing, but Aisha was wary of his manner and his intent was clear. She did not want him to touch her. He grabbed for her wrists as she tried to scramble past him and she winced in agony as he clamped a firm hold over her newly healed wounds. His breath was warm on her neck as he pulled her close, his lips lightly touching an ear and then her cheek. It made her nauseous and she struggled; that only made him hold her tighter, closer and his voice came in a hiss when he finally spoke.

"I can give you everything and you fight me? I am Prince Emir and I get what I want. It will be so much easier if you just give in." He smiled with an eastern charm but his eyes were piercing, almost cruel as if to warn her of the consequences of refusing a master in the Sultan's palace.

"But I do not want everything and I did not ask to be brought here." She spat upon him and pulled one arm loose but mid strike he grabbed her and pulled her roughly to him. Her actions angered him further.

"Now I will take what I want and you will get nothing in return."

He threw her back on the bed, pinning her arms over her head with one hand, and with the other, he ripped the front of her dress. Aisha screamed. He raised a hand to silence her but stopped, as a stream of light from outside suddenly shone through an opening in the draped curtains.

"Haidar! What do you want? Leave us."

"I will not leave you to do your will upon a mere child. Now, let her go."

"Dare you speak to me that way, brother? I will have you beheaded."

"And so you have threatened and I am still here, *dear* brother. Now, let her go." Haidar pushed Emir aside and extended a hand to Aisha. She hesitated.

"Forgive me, young one, for looking so much like your attacker, but I am his twin brother and for that I am truly sorry. I am not, however, of the same flawed cloth. Our father taught us both well, but Emir chose to value treachery over treasure."

His words had not only wisdom, but compassion; he did not have to say more to convince her she would be safe. He held out his hand – it was warm and gentle on her skin as he cloaked her in a velvet cape, wrapping it around her shoulders, leading her safely from the alcove past the angered Emir.

"Brother, you test my love for you." Emir's hand held firm Haidar's upper arm; their eyes met and there was silence. For a moment, Aisha feared there would be a fight and she imagined a long blade killing her dashing hero.

She stopped, but not before the thoughts of where she might end up entered her mind, and she felt the nausea rise again with a rush of cold sweat over her body. Her vision dimmed and, although she fought against it, the heat of the fever hit and she felt her knees weaken.

Watching the light from the hundreds of candles fade from her sight, she fell.

Aisha awoke, tucked into a wool layered bed, a cool cloth on her forehead. A young girl smiled as she reapplied the compress with fresh water and touched Aisha's forehead.

"Fever – no."

"Where am I?"

Aisha struggled to sit up and looked around the room, suddenly panicked. Unlike her last accommodations, however, this room was clean and richly furnished with dark accents and white gauze curtains. The stone floor was scattered with a woven silk tapestries, similar to the one thrown across the bottom of the large canopy bed.

"You are safe here. You are a guest of Prince Haidar."

"I am in his home? Is this his bed, too?"

The young girl looked confused, and then shook her head. "No. No. You do not have to worry – he is truly a prince and a gentleman – unlike his brother." The girl patted Aisha's arm and encouraged her to lie back. "Rest. You are safe here."

The girl rose and brought a tray to the bedside. "You must be hungry, now eat... then rest. There is a room with a bath," she pointed to an arched doorway, "...when you feel like it." She turned to leave and Aisha touched her hand.

"Thank you." The girl smiled and was gone.

Aisha sat up on the edge of the bed. The fruit on the tray looked appealing, but another set of items caught her eye, instead. An intricately carved hair brush and matching mirror lay side by side on the tray. The matte silver finish had black etchings and the back of the mirror depicted a garden scene with a young girl walking alongside a lion; there was a smile on the girl's beautiful face. Aisha picked up the mirror and fingered the engraved detail. Her family could not afford such luxuries. Its price would most likely feed them for the whole winter season. She turned it over, reluctantly viewing her reflection, and knowing she was from a mere peasant family, her thoughts were confused. *Did she have the right to enjoy such comfort even if it were offered at the hands of her captors?*

She touched her cheek, watching intently as the girl in the mirror did the same. She saw her own eyes staring back at her and decided she would allow herself this one enjoyment. She picked up the silver brush and as she pulled it through her hair, she smiled into the mirror.

In there, she thought, *is another life*.

Chapter 7 – A Lion's Courage

Aaslan continued to stumble through the trees without care to the noise he made while clambering over deadfall and stomping through last fall's leaves, thick in spots, the top layer just barely dried in the late spring warmth. The only thing he was mindful of was direction, and he concentrated on a parallel course with the road even while in full cover of the trees.

"Are you going to trek three days through the trees?" Udmurt's low, monotone voice carried to him from the road. He glanced, still angered, toward the sound and caught a glimpse of Hazine plodding along, keeping even with his labored steps.

"Leave. Go your own way – this is not your journey." Aaslan's voice quivered and he shouted louder than he knew he should. Udmurt's words came back to him ... *focus on getting there first...* and he was immediately sorry for his actions. To give away their position in this forest was sure death. He knew nothing of survival.

"Quiet, boy. You want the Rogues to know you are after them? The whole northern forest now knows where you are by the way you shout." The rumble of wheels followed along after Udmurt's horse, and Aaslan realized they were now not just two; Izmir walked closely behind the cart holding the harness reins in his gloved hand and in the other, the leather lead of a small saddled pack horse.

Aaslan felt shame as he realized what and who his survival depended upon. He emerged from the trees beside the pair on the road and stood for a moment as he tried to formulate some kind of explanation.

As he struggled to express his feelings, he realized they were not interested in hearing or receiving them. Udmurt continued on, with a wink, and just waved a hand to follow.

"She's yours now."

Izmir handed the reins to Aaslan and, without ceremony, continued after Udmurt.

Aaslan felt relief and remorse all in one moment, but swallowed back the little boy tears that threatened. The two men did not need to hear his pitiful explanations nor did they need to see the weakness in him that seemed so easy to follow. He wondered if it was their company that brought out this dependency. He had steeled his determination that first night alone in the forest, knowing his duty was to his sister, and the future lay ahead of him no matter what danger accompanied it or where it took him. He stroked the mare's forehead as she nuzzled him, eager to keep up with the rest of the group. The pair caught up with their companions, Aaslan with an assumed grown up stride.

As darkness fell, they came upon a small clearing to one side of the road and Udmurt lead them through and into the dense thicket bordering its far edges. What seemed to be a thick barrier fell away easy to let both man and beast through. On the other side of a grassy knoll was a bottom land camp hidden from the road. A sheltered cutaway was hollowed into the hill where a fire could be lit for warmth or cooking without giving away their location by the flames. The high bank served as a wind break and it was considerably warmer than the open road. Izmir was able to pull the wagon into the clearing by way of a gradually inclined pathway. The men tied their horses to the trees nearby.

Without discussion, they pulled wrapped furs from their packs to line the ground near the fire pit and gathered wood and kindling from the surrounding trees. Aaslan watched and bent to gather chips of bark and small wind scattered limbs that he piled along the bank by the fire. He took the flint Udmurt handed him without question and proceeded to spark the small pile of dried brush he gathered to the center of the pit. He felt relief and a hidden swell of pride as the fuel ignited with little effort. He shielded the small flame with his hand and gently blew encouragement into it.

"Good job."

It was a quiet accolade from Udmurt but a welcome one; Aaslan felt a calming veil embrace him as he settled in to sit close to the warmth of the fire. The two men soon joined him, handing him a piece of dried pastirma, as they passed a leather flask between them. The faint smell of liquor permeated his nostrils, but he just chewed happily on his jerky, trying not to judge.

"Drink?"

Izmir offered the vessel to Aaslan who just shook his head, knowing he was still boy enough to refuse, not yet man enough to stomach the strong Russian vodka. Izmir just grunted, and did not insist, as he took another swig from the spout.

"Suit yourself."

The ease of the evening settled over the man as he drained the drink without further word. Reclining on one elbow, Izmir closed his eyes, his head lolled to one side. Aaslan was unsure if the man was sleeping or just very quiet.

Udmurt arose and walked over to the base of a huge tree where he knelt within the light of the fire ring. He reached inside what appeared to be a hollow. Aaslan did not feel like leaving the comfort of the fire and fur, after the long day's trek, just to find out what the hunter might be up to. The strain of reaching far inside showed on Udmurt's face, and Aaslan watched as he moved his arm inside, past the elbow, straining further.

"Arrrgh..." Udmurt groaned in his attempt to pull his arm free and swore, gritting his teeth. Aaslan jumped up.

"Never mind, boy, just caught up on a root..." There was a tearing sound and Udmurt wrenched his arm free. "Damn. This is my best shirt, too." He grinned up at Aaslan, and stopped, a confused look on his face. "What? You trying to scare me now? You know I am not going to fall for your feeble attempts to get back at me..." He realized Aaslan was not listening to him, but was focused on the brush behind him at the edge of the lighted clearing. His trained ear picked up the snorting, snuffling sounds and he did not have to turn to see the wild boar.

In a flash, Aaslan took up the sleeping Izmir's sword and charged the clearing toward the animal that now closed in on Udmurt. The angered sow was intent on killing the man, but when he rolled out of the way in time, he was no longer her destined target. Aaslan pierced the three hundred pound animal, skewered upon the blade as the two met almost head on at full run. The boy barely missed the sharp canines as she threw her head up to bite him. His grasp on the handle slipped. He landed in the dirt on the other side of her. Her shrill scream woke Izmir and he watched as she slumped to her death barely a foot from him.

"Supper." He grinned, unshaken.

Udmurt pulled Aaslan to his feet. Their eyes met and with a nervous laugh, he pulled the young warrior into a thankful hug. Aaslan knew he would no longer be regarded as merely a boy and his companions would refrain from testing him. He was aware of his growth; survival was sure.

The night feast was a welcome one for celebration.

Chapter 8 – A Brother's Honor

Aisha followed her companion's lead and held the lace shawl close to her chin as they strolled the covered bazaar protected from the heat of the noon day sun. They paused at each market stall to peruse the merchant's goods – silk from far off lands, silver rings, shiny brass pots with loose fitting lids, hand woven tapestries – and each time they moved away just shaking their heads in silent answer to the calls of the vendors. The dark skinned men eyed the girls from a distance but none chanced more.

"There are so many beautiful things. I have not seen this many choices all in one place. I am so happy we are allowed out to see the market. I did not think Prince Haidar would be so trusting."

"Oh, it is me he trusts; do not for a moment think he is not watching."

Aisha lifted her eyes to the surrounding walled enclosure, blinking into the bright sunlight that streamed through high arched windows as she scanned the doorways and wall recesses.

"Surely, we would see him then?"

"It might not be he who watches."

"So why did he let us go then?"

"Prince Haidar likes you, little one, and wants you to be happy. Here, this would please him." Saharra held up a soft rose colored scarf to Aisha's fair skin and smiled.

"And why would I want to please him? If he likes me so much, why does he not just let me go?"

Saharra put the scarf back on the table and bowed, lowering her eyes as she shook her head and turned away. She held the young girl's elbow and they moved away from the table to the cover of a brightly colored awning.

"Prince Haidar is not your enemy. You must believe he saved you from a fate worse than death."

"I am thankful for his help and he has certainly been a most gracious host."

"You must realize your debt to him."

"But are you not with him?"

Saharra stopped and with a slight, amused smile she shook her head; she laid a soft hand alongside Aisha's cheek as she spoke.

"You are a beautiful vision – a young girl, naïve, as I once was..." Her voice trailed off and there was a fleeting sadness in her eyes. "Prince Haidar is my brother. I stay with him because he looks out for me and protects me and it is my duty, therefore, to serve him." Aisha's shocked look quickened her continued response. "Not in his bed - as his house servant. Your naivety is refreshing but I am afraid it will fade."

"Is it always a sister's duty to serve her brother, here...? I mean, in..." Aisha's confusion brought another smile to Saharra's face and she tightened her grip on the girl's elbow, leading her back into the crowd.

"Not in the sultan's palace, but circumstances are so for me." With her answer, she quickly changed the subject. "So you now know my brother, tell me... what is your brother like?"

Upon their return to the Prince's residence, a young boy ran from the doorway, one fist clutching tightly a piece of torn paper, and in the other hand a gold coin flashed in the sunlight, pinched between two fingers.

"What say you, young master?"

"A message for the Prince, nothing more." He kept on running.

Inside, Prince Haidar awaited their return, and he called them into the sitting room, offering them some water. He patted the cushion next to him and motioned for Aisha to sit; Saharra sat across from them.

"Did you enjoy your outing at the market?"

"Yes, thank you, though we did not buy much." Aisha was almost apologetic as if their enjoyment of the day actually depended upon exotic purchases to please the prince. *Perhaps, the Prince would let her return again tomorrow to buy that scarf Saharra thought he'd like.* As if reading her thoughts, Prince Haidar quelled any hope of returning to the market.

"That is unfortunate, as I cannot have you wandering the streets again. I hear tell of a traveler who speared a rushing wild boar with one thrust of his sword, killing it in its tracks."

The girls looked to one another, questioning the relevance of the news Haidar shared with them.

"Brother that has naught to do with us. Why should we be kept from the market?"

"Oh but it does, my dear sister, because it appears another brother looks out for his sister, too. Do you not know your brother, Aaslan, searches for you?" He grasped Aisha's hand and she did not pull away. Their eyes met and she felt that strange sensation stir again inside her, only this time she was not overcome with nausea and instead felt her face grow warm. Still, she did not pull her hand away, and managed a small laugh.

"That cannot be my brother, although, I am certain in my heart he searches for me."

"It is one and the same."

"My brother does not slay wild boars. He cannot hook a worm to catch a fish without my help. He surely could not skewer a charging boar upon a sword." She shook her head. "No, it cannot be one and the same."

"I have it on good advice that it is he, traveling with two mountain men. They are at this moment headed to the city of Istanbul. This nemesis will not be one to fool with."

"I cannot believe it is, but if it is, then let it be so. Please, Prince Haidar, do not harm him for he only seeks to find me." Her voice softened and the pleading left as she continued with certainty. "You cannot fault a brother for wanting to save his sister."

Saharra's eyes met her brother's quick glance in her direction as he let go of Aisha's hand. He stood and began to pace, rubbing his forehead and shaking his head.

"Let not your brother come for glory as a brother should serve his sister based only upon his love for her and what is right."

"He would come for me because he loves me. He would search for me until the end. If this story is true and he slew a charging boar he would do that deed for friendship or love or survival - not glory. It is not in his heart to need to serve, only to love."

Sahara remained quiet while her brother paced and Aisha noticed there were tears in her eyes. She stood solemnly and faced Aisha.

"Some brothers do not do what is right or what is love and some brothers now live with that guilt in their heart. But at least he can say he did what he did for the glory, in the name of the family, even though he did not do what he should." Tears rolled unchecked and Aisha realized that Haidar, too, was silently crying, his head bowed.

"Your brother Aaslan is as brave as the name he bears; and your brother slew the beast while my brother let him live." Sahara ran from the room.

Chapter 9 – Haunting

"That beast was a worthy feast, young Aaslan." Udmurt moaned his appreciation while he picked remnants of meat from his teeth with a sliver of deadwood and laid back, his head resting on one arm.

"We shan't go hungry for some time now, I should think." Aaslan reclined on the fur bedroll and groaned. The excitement of the kill brought pleasant thoughts to him reminding him that no longer would the men consider him a mere boy. He earned his way and their respect by the feat of what he thought was bravery. Udmurt was still cautious in his proclamations.

"Foolhardy actions – but a worthy prize, indeed."

Aaslan saw the hint of a smile curl at the corners of the older man's lips and he did not argue the point with him. In his heart he knew this deed was equal to many endured by boys during their rite of passage into manhood. He was now worthy of the name he bore. Izmir let out a satisfying belch that echoed through the still night air and Aaslan chuckled to himself.

Suddenly, Udmurt jumped up from his spot near the fire and Aaslan's blood drained from his face, fear soon shattered the bravery badge he just pinned upon himself.

"What?"

"'Tis fine lad, I just forgot in all this glory of battle what I went to that damned tree for in the first place."

Aaslan's breath slowly exhaled and he tried to steady his quivering knees. He did not want the men to know the thought of being brave again felt worse than the unknowing. If it was expected of him, he might not perform quite so well next time.

Udmurt was on the ground at the hollow in the large tree and cautiously peered into the darkness before stretching a long, muscled arm upward into the tree trunk. This time, he pulled from it a bundled wrap of worn cloth bound with leather ties. He smiled as he cradled the handful close to his body and sat back down in the light of the campfire. Izmir was now asleep. Udmurt spoke quietly.

"I do not need to know you in any other way more than what I have already witnessed to know I want to do this - even so, I do not know why I am propelled to offer you this gift. There is something about your determination that reminds me... of me, once upon a time." He caught Aaslan's slight smile and continued with a laugh, "Oh, you think I was always this assured of myself? Nay, I was a lad, too, and can relate to the journey you partake in – not by choice – but by need." He extended the wrapped package to Aaslan. "I want you to have this in case you need it to find or buy a happy ending to the search for your sister."

Aaslan took the package and bit his lip, determined the newly adorned man would not cry little boy tears. It was difficult, not because of the gift and its meaning, but because he was afraid to think what might be required to find his sister, let alone save her and return her back home. He had not the time before then to think on the possibilities and the drive to keep up to a trail that quickly grew cold, never allowed him the opportunity. All that mattered was staying on the right course.

He pulled the leather ties and the rough burlap cloth fell away to reveal a small carved box with a hinged lid. He looked up at Udmurt and lifted the cover at his nod. Inside, lay stacks of gold coins – there had to be at least two dozen. Aaslan leaned closer to the fire to allow more light on the box and the metal gleamed in the fiery glow.

"I cannot… accept this." Aaslan's eyes were wide and he stumbled on the words.

"You surely can and will." Udmurt reached over and cupped a large hand on Aaslan's shoulder. "I know what it is like to try to find someone and with this gift I guarantee your quest will be successful. Believe me; nothing speaks like gold to the slave traders." He patted the boy's shoulder, then withdrew his arm and lay back, closing his eyes. "Get some sleep, brave one, for we ride before dawn."

Aaslan rewrapped the box and tied the leather binding tight around it. He shoved it inside the bag he carried and covered it with the hide; it was a comforting pillow for his head. He was always determined to find Aisha, there was no doubt. Now, he also knew he not only had help but the means to buy back something that was a real treasure, even more so than gold coins – his sister. That night, he willed himself to a much needed sleep and dreamt of her rescue.

His bronze skin was striking against the stark white of the robes that flowed around him in layers of silken cloth woven with golden threads. Crisscrossed stitches embossed the entire edge of the fabric intertwined with bay leaves and jasmine, the official flower of the kingdom. A hooded cloak covered his head. His hair was jet black and it matched the magnificent Arabian stallion he sat astride. Both were regal in their stance. A gentle Turkish breeze ruffled the horse's mane and tail and he pranced ever so slightly, as if dancing upon the sand. The sun was warm and there were footprints leading away from him. The Prince dismounted and followed.

A girl's laughter rang like crystal bells in a still chamber – fleeting, almost hollow but pristine and with the innocence of young years. The amber colored veils cloaked her body and a beaded headdress protected her fair skin and auburn hair from the sun's rays. She twirled amongst the sand, arms outstretched and face upturned. The Prince caught her by the arm and fell to his knees in front of her pushing the protective cloak back off of his head. In his hand was a silver box, a lion carved upon the lid lying in the shade of a bay tree.

As she opened the lid, the sun glinted across the facets of an amber jewel casting sparkles like the joy reflected in her eyes. The silken veil fell away from her face and she smiled. With faint pink lips and crimson blush, she kissed the Prince and he swept her up into his arms.

"You will be my wife."

"Aisha! No!" Aaslan sat bolt upright. The campfire was now just ash and the faint light of dawn was breaking in the eastern sky.

"It is okay, brave one, time to ride. We will find your sister." Udmurt pulled Aaslan to his feet and handed him the reins to his horse. "It was just a bad dream."

Chapter 10 – The Quilt

By the time Aisha excused herself with a respectful bow to Prince Haidar, and made her way to the solace of her bed chamber, Saharra's composure had returned. Aisha was concerned for the girl who offered her safety and companionship, but was curious, too. *What caused the emotional outburst directed toward the Prince?* Aisha was also surprised at Prince Haidar's obvious distress with his sister's words and blatant accusations.

Biting her lip, Aisha took up the crest adorned brush, and pulled it thoughtfully through her long auburn hair. She watched Saharra, who tended to her duties, yet remained quiet for the longest time. When she did speak, she chose her words, carefully.

"Your brother, the Prince... he loves you, you know. I see the same protectiveness my brother offers me and he loves me no end."

Saharra stopped, long enough to stare at the young girl. She, too, found composure and sureness in a delayed response. "I do not doubt his love - now - but there was a time when I hated him. A brother with a vow to do so must protect his charge at all cost." She stopped suddenly, chasing a tearful memory to the back of her mind. "The cost was mine to bear, and he did not do his duty." Saharra held up a hand, anticipating young Aisha's next question. "It does not matter what was done, or what was not done. It is all in the past now and nothing can change the past. I am thankful, though, he makes amends every day of his life. He has now earned his sister's love."

Sahara smiled, content to let go of the conversation directed toward her. Eager to speak highly of Haidar, she diverted Aisha's curiosity to the present. "So, you like my brother?"

"He is a handsome man, and I assume he is of the image most little girls might conjure up if asked to describe their prince, yet, I am cautious to his intent."

Saharra laughed. "Did you age twenty years of wisdom in your short visit?"

Aisha blushed, not knowing if Saharra chided her as a naïve girl or if she found some foolishness in her answer. "I would like him better if he would let me go."

"I meant you no disrespect, Aisha. My comment merely was that you are wise beyond your years."

"Why does he hold onto someone like a possession? I am not his to keep."

"He will prove himself an honorable man and do what is necessary when the time comes."

"Will he respect my brother's honor, too? Will he spare his life? If Aaslan comes to take me home, and I know in my heart he will try, will the Prince let me go? Will he let Aaslan live?"

"I cannot say and, although I admire your brother's bravery, I do hope he approaches with the stealth and cunning of the lion he has proved to be so far."

Aisha felt a renewed pride for her brother, at that moment, yet a secret fear tugged at her heart. *I must not worry for his well being,* she thought, knowing that concentration on her own survival was still necessary. She must be observant and commit all details to her memory for safe keeping. She watched as Saharra folded the blankets that lay strewn across the foot of the bed. Aisha noticed among them a particularly heavy one - woven through with thick woollen tufts.

"That is a beautiful quilt," Aisha said, pointing to the earth-toned cover.

"It belonged to my mother. She made it when she was just a young girl and gave it to me when I was only a baby."

Aisha looked around the room - woven silk tapestries, bed clothes of the finest Middle Eastern textiles – and, as little as she knew from her backwoods schooling, she knew that finery adorned this room, not rough hewn quilts of heavy cloth with plant dyed wools.

"That quilt is not from here."

"Whatever do you mean?" Saharra's alarm showed, as she hugged the precious quilt to her body. "It is mine."

"I do not doubt that it is yours, Saharra. I merely mean, it is of Russian composition - those colors and fabric. They are not from here. The hands of a Turkish princess did not make such a gift."

Chapter 11 – The Eastern Jewel

On the eve of the summer solstice, Aaslan and his travel companions crested the hill on the final leg of the journey into Istanbul. Although he had been frantic to make it into the city before the traders set sail for the next port, Aaslan reined in his mount and sat quietly in awe. A disturbing peace washed over him which he could not justify. The calm that engulfed his senses was in direct competition to the knot, tying and untying itself, in the pit of his stomach.

The eastern jewel had forever been his dream but now it was no more than a necessity. The Mecca shimmered radiant silver in the mid-day sun; a haze of heat hung loosely over the distant horizon. It appeared to fade in and out, like his thoughts. A gentle breeze, almost non-existent, played at the strands of loose hair about his face.

Droplets of sweat traced dirt patterns down Aaslan's forehead and he mopped absentmindedly at them with the sleeve of his tunic. He could not take his eyes from the sight before him for fear it might shimmer, fade, and disappear. At times on the road, he thought they would never get to their destination, but now, he was not imagining this long sought forbidden oasis. The anxiety in his stomach began to rise and he choked back the sour threat of bile with a quick swig from the water flask at his side.

"She is a beauty from up here."

Udmurt's horse nudged close, shaking Aaslan from his trance. He swallowed hard realizing the meaning in his friend's statement.

"It is real then." His statement was more a vocal confirmation to the truth than a too obvious question. "You have been to Istanbul?" Aaslan realized that for a traveler like Udmurt that it was another too obvious question. He half expected to receive no answer.

"Ah, yes." The rough man's words caught, as he continued, slowly. "Yes… but that was many years ago and I have not since stepped foot in the city."

"Will we make it into the city before dark?"

"No – you do not want to go in until dark." Aaslan's sure to be voiced concerns were cut short with a quick follow up as Udmurt waved a cautious hand. "We have our guide with us." Izmir rattled up the pathway behind them. "In fact, we should get off the roadway. At this vantage point, it will not be long before we are discovered."

Udmurt followed Izmir's lead as he pulled the cart off into the hard grassy mounds flanking the eastern edge of the road. They disappeared into the trees. Aaslan followed reluctantly.

Even though he respected Udmurt's advice and realized the older man knew best, his sense of urgency was returning. He had to find Aisha. The dream that haunted his sleep of late felt too real to be ignored. His dilemma lay with the hope that it was true – *at least if his sister was with a prince, she would not be sold into the hands of an ill-favored master.*

With a gentle kick to the ribs of his pony, Aaslan urged his mount from the exposed road and disappeared into the shadows of the trees. It was beyond his trusting beliefs to think the ill-favored master and the prince could be one and the same.

Chapter 12 – The Map

For all her earned wisdom despite her young years, Aisha did not know why her words hurt Saharra. She was really only pointing out something she knew to be true given the details of her surroundings and her keen sense of observation. *The quilt was not from here.* She meant no disrespect, but it was obvious that the older girl took offence to the statement.

"You know nothing about it."

"Saharra, I am sorry if I upset you." Aisha reached out a comforting hand that was promptly swatted away. "I did not mean to hurt you. I am truly sorry."

Aisha's sincerity melted into quiet resolve as she retreated to the bayed alcove in their shared room. There, in the warmth of the sun, she sat looking out over the tops of the nearby trees to the distant hills. Her thoughts moved from the girl in the room, the prince and his palace, the busy markets and traded treasure, to the forest. Somewhere, out there, she knew her brother would be searching.

It was only a few moments before she felt the warmth of Saharra's hand on her shoulder. Aisha turned toward her, tears fresh in her eyes.

"You are young, but I forget how wise you have proven to be." Saharra sat alongside Aisha on the large satin covered cushion. "I never really considered my gift to be out of place amongst the riches in the palace." She shook her head. "I just do not know why I did not notice it before – perhaps..." She stopped. She, too, had tears in her eyes.

"It is a connection to someone special whom you have lost."

"I have not had anyone who considered it important to talk to me about my mother and how I may be feeling without her."

"I can relate in more ways than you think. I was taken from mine and I am here with you instead of with her."

As their eyes met, there was a moment of realization for both girls – an understanding that could only be explained by their forced companionship.

"Oh." Saharra closed her eyes, still holding the treasured quilt close to her. When she opened them she grabbed Aisha's hand and smiled.

"What?"

"I have something to show you."

With the confidence of sharing a secret she knew would not be revealed, Saharra offered to Aisha the one thing only a true friend would offer – the key to freedom. At that moment, Aisha knew there was something different about this princess. All prior evidence in her behavior confirmed an undying devotion to a brother who, at some point in the past, was derelict in his duties to protect her, yet revealed a courage struggling to escape.

"What is it?"

Saharra retrieved a tiny rolled parchment hidden from beneath the layers of silk tapestries hung on the stone walls of the room. It was small enough that not even under close scrutiny would it have been discovered. Aisha moved closer as Saharra opened the paper, carefully.

"It is a map."

"To what?"

"It leads to the forest beyond the city – underground." Saharra traced the tunnel from the west side of the palace leading to the eastern edge of Marmara Sea that bordered Istanbul. There the map stopped abruptly – the torn edge ragged and weathered with age.

"The forest – where? How do you know? It is not a whole map." The feelings of hope slowly receded.

"I have been through the tunnels as a young girl, playing..." Saharra stopped abruptly, her voice fading as a painful memory passed through her mind. She rolled the map back to its tiny roll and quickly tucked it inside the folds of her muslin wrap. "We will talk of this another time."

Progress through the trees was slow and soon after their departure from the road, Izmir abandoned the cart, leaving it hidden in a dense thicket covered with deadfall. They would retrieve it on their journey back. Aaslan found comfort in that declaration.

The wind picked up over the course of the afternoon and the travelers were spared the heat of the sun. It amazed Aaslan how quiet three horses with riders could be when you listened to the noises of the forest all around you. Snuffling boars burrowing through the undergrowth provided welcome cover for their trek even though they brought shivers of recollection to Aaslan. He kept a steady pace with the two men and a keen, though nervous eye, on the shadows falling around them as they moved closer to nightfall and their destination.

"We will camp here until the late hours of the night." Izmir's voice was low as he slid from his horse. He pulled the pack and his gear from her back, unhitched the harness leads for the wagon and let her free.

"What are you doing?" Aaslan's whisper was sharp and fearful. He learned not too far back on the road that spoken words were not your comfort if given too loudly. He did not, however, realize the reasons for Izmir's actions given they still had travel ahead of them.

"Our journey continues on foot. The beasts will find us when we need them."

Aaslan did not pursue what he did not know despite his obvious doubt. He patted Silniy, his dependable mare, on the neck and followed suit. With a knowing nuzzle to his cheek, she moved off quietly into the trees, leaving him to question his vulnerability on foot in the depths of the wilds.

"You will be fine. Let us set up camp and rest for awhile. No fire, but at least we have jerky and ale." Udmurt spread his bedroll over the ground and settled in, chewing on a strip of the dried meat.

"This is where we will enter the city." In the waning light, Izmir pointed to a circled spot on a worn piece of parchment he pulled from a leather pouch hidden inside his pack. It looked to be just inside the edge of the forest nearest to the city and running along the eastern shores of the Sea of Marmara. The Turkish countryside was well known to travelers, but the obvious route was new to Udmurt.

"Pizdets na khui blyad!"

"Oy!"

As quickly as the men's verbal discharge began, it accelerated into a heated physical match on the cold ground. Each man wielded his share of blows upon the other while each took equal punishment in return. Aaslan's shock quickly became action as he rescued the endangered map from amidst the tussle.

"Udmurt!" The din of fight could not keep the sound of the Russian man's name from echoing through the approaching dusk.

"Shush, boy!"

"Do not shush me."

Aaslan's anger and courage took over as he confronted the men. He held the map toward them as they pulled stray leaves from their beards and hair. "How do you know the tunnel goes into the city? How can you possibly know?"

Aaslan indicated to the edge of the map where it stopped abruptly, the torn edge ragged and weathered with age.

Chapter 13 – Question of Loyalty

The night was cold and Aaslan awoke to the howl of night dogs just after midnight. A soggy mist covered the forest and it reminded him of that first day when he determined the trail and tracked the direction of his quarry. He lay still, and then dared to shift quietly on the rooted dirt in his hidden grassy bed under the overhanging boughs. The trio welcomed sleep soon after the disagreement and the men grew silent and ignored each other. The map was put to safe keeping as quickly as it was drawn. All knew without vocalization that their journey and their duty would bring a return to their camaraderie; it had done so before so there was no reason to assume regrets or hard feelings. That was just the way of the road.

The fog was the perfect accompanying shield for moving closer to the city under cloak of darkness. The moon added just enough of a glow to provide light in open areas. If the scouts or palace guards were out, they would have a hard time detecting the trained trackers on foot.

Aaslan grew to trust the older men over the course of their exchange but also grew to trust his own instincts even though they often came upon him with little warning. He felt his father would be proud that all the lessons taught actually amounted to more than just words. His actions would speak loudly for his character back in the village. Their family was well respected but a son always had to do his part to bring honor to the clan. His body ached with the night dampness, a minor setback; for he knew the ache in his heart would surely kill him if his mission was not fulfilled. They were so close now. They would soon be bringing Aisha home.

Aaslan sat up as he heard the men next to him stir. He was eager to continue.

Saharra brought the map out again for Aisha to study. It was early the next morning and the sun was a shimmering gold sliver in the misty sky.

"You need to know this without fail - the tunnels are dark in places and one wrong turn can put you somewhere you do not want to be." The warning in the girl's voice came through clear and as their eyes met, Aisha saw the pain she heard creep into Saharra's voice the night before. It was pain enough to silence her for the rest of the evening and Aisha was surprised she would bring the subject up again so soon.

"You must gather only what you need and what you can carry."

"You forget, I came here with very little." Aisha's words were meant as naïve truth, but they jabbed Saharra like a knife.

"You will take of mine what you need to survive - I owe you that, at the very least."

"You did nothing to cause my grief and have always been there to take care of me; I therefore, owe you my gratitude. You do not even have to do this, but yet you are helping me to find a way out of here." Aisha took the older girl by the shoulders and a sudden thought came to her. "You will come with me."

Aisha retrieved a linen drawstring bag hidden out of sight along the far edge of the bed. Before anything else, she wrapped Saharra's quilt into a tight roll and pushed it into the bottom of the pouch. The sweater, she wore the first night in the cave cellars, was a soft wrap for the precious silver hair brush and mirror. She glanced up as doubt overcame her bold assumption.

"They are yours."

Saharra smiled and put an arm around the young girl's shoulder. "Take them as my gift. You know I cannot leave with you, my place is with my brother in the palace, but I will see you out of the tunnels before I make my way back." She held a hand up to silence Aisha's protest and pushed a wayward curl off of her forehead. "You have taught me more in this short time than all my years and I will be forever grateful to you."

Aisha gave Saharra a hug, out of respect and for confirmation of their friendship, but also to hide her tears. She was unsure at that moment but suspected they were born of disappointment.

Udmurt, true to Aaslan's expectations, did not bring up the map again. In fact, Aaslan would be hard pressed to find fault or deviation from the trail he studied on the map the night before. He suspected it was not the first time the mountain man made his way to the Mecca city underground, despite his enraged claims. With the treasured box of coins wrapped tightly in the middle of his pack roll, he slung it over his back and strapped it close for unhindered movement through the trees. Aaslan felt success was sure, as if on the tips of his fingers.

The three men moved steadily and with stealth through the trees until they came to a trail that crossed the road and headed closer to the Sea of Marmara. There, they would come to a cave-like entryway. In timed and silent precision, one by one they crouched then crossed the roadway and disappeared into the shrub cover along the marshy shores. Progress slowed but it was necessary to ensure their position was not discovered. With measured motion, they moved from one safe spot to the next, until Aaslan saw the doorway to what he thought was the final leg of his journey. *I am here, my sister*, he thought as he awaited Udmurt's signal.

Prince Haidar rode out that morning on his favorite mount, a regal black Arabian stallion, named Sultan. He had no reason to suspect the girls would not be in the palace upon his return. His sister was loyal to him and Aisha, over the course of her confinement, had come to accept her situation. He had grown quite fond of her. In fact, it was his intent to take her for his bride; his one and only bride for, unlike his brother, he believed in only one true love.

He also had no reason to look back to the palace as his spirited mount galloped away. If he had he might have noticed the two girls, watching for his departure from the window of their room, hidden from discovery behind the safety of the drawn gauze curtains.

Chapter 14 – In the Belly of the Underground

Aaslan blinked, adjusting the focus of his vision to the shadows, just inside the first turn of the tunnel. Daylight from the cave opening faded quickly as he and the men disappeared in silent precision into the under belly of the countryside. Stories filtered through the Turkish culture of lost societies having lived and long since been buried deep beneath the Mecca jewel. Aaslan wondered of their need for such seclusion. It was a cellar fortress and at one time considered safe haven and escape for those caught within what they perceived as a less than perfect life. That was until the Rogues claimed it to be their turf and although they gleaned roads and travelers of their precious cargo, the underground tunnels offered vaults for safe keeping.

Up ahead along the six foot wide passage way, Aaslan could make out the faint glow of a lantern mounted on the stone wall. It would make travel easier in some respects, and more dangerous in others, for they could hurry in undiscovered movements along the shadows, but the dilemma lay in crossing those beams of light. Hurry upright and chance discovery, or crawl and be ambushed while compromised.

With a silent understanding between them borne of instinct, they ran, abrupt in stopping just beyond the circle of light. They held a collective breath until it was certain no other sound could be heard.

"Two hundred yards ahead, just beyond the next lantern, the tunnel meets a crossroad..." Udmurt whispered in husky tones, easily hitting his companion's ears with instruction.

Listening to the man's words, Aaslan readjusted his own doubts as he did not remember seeing a cross cutting tunnel on the map.

"To the right lives certain death, for the Rogues make that direction home." Udmurt's voice dropped lower yet. "Left... disappears into the sea – it is meant as a trap for those who venture into the unknown, unwelcome, and as a safeguard for those who know the tunnels. Straight ahead is our pathway to the city where we will arrive just beyond the view of the palace guards, but so close to the covered market place we will be able to melt into the mid-day crowds."

Aaslan's stomach churned with a heightened sensation that housed a mix of fear, excitement, and raw victory. He knew in his heart – *he could almost taste it* - his determined desire and his companion's brute strength, would bind them to completing the next leg of the journey, quickly and without confrontation. Udmurt's words confirmed his suspicions that the man had at some point been in the tunnel for his description was too sure to be conjecture. Aaslan steadied his battle weary knees and firmed the grip upon the knife presented to him at their midnight departure. He was uncertain of his ability to use it on another human being, but if he focused on saving his sister, he knew he could be forced to do what was necessary in order to rescue her.

Chapter 15 – No Time to Waste

As Prince Haidar disappeared over the rise in the trail extending from the palace entryway; Saharra stepped back from the window, in silence. *It is time*, she thought, as she realized she would be betraying her brother. She could not, however, reveal any hesitation or fear to Aisha – the girl must escape and she needed her help to do so. *How telling – to help one brother means to disobey another?*

"Come, there is no time to waste. The Prince does not venture off too long on hot days. He values his prize stallion far too much to risk his well being in the heat. It is early, but he will return before the noon day sun is overhead." She tied her long dark hair back to the nape of her neck with a leather tie and offered one to Aisha. They pulled dark berry ink dyed hooded tunics over their light gauze dresses and slipped their feet into soft hide slippers. The fabric would ensure warmth yet allow the girls the silence they needed to steal away.

Saharra ushered the younger girl ahead of her and grasped the travel bag firmly by the ties. Stone steps at the end of the upper level hallway led to the lower level, and then proceeded further to another, then another. Grey shadows soon became blackened as the light from the upper chambers faded. Aisha felt the cool air escaping from the depths below and she welcomed the change from the hot air of the palace. She also welcomed the challenge that lay ahead. Saharra's grasp on her hand was tight and she followed as if sure of her step, trusting the lead of her rescuer. She could see lanterns at intervals ahead, casting faint light across the passage way. Her outstretched hand steadied her hurried silent footsteps and she felt comfort as her fingers grazed the stone containment.

Saharra slowed as they approached the first lantern and Aisha matched her pace, until they came to a complete stop, still hidden just inside the border of darkness.

"We must wait until we are completely sure we will not be detected."

"How far do these tunnels reach?" Aisha whispered back, even though she was aware that conversation was out of place. Her curiosity dictated the need to know what lay beyond. She pushed her wayward curls back over her shoulder as she leaned close to the wall peering down the passage way.

"Whatever you do, do not take a cross passage. You must remain on this one, straight, always."

There was warning in the answer and although it did not address her question, Aisha knew there was a message to be heeded. Saharra knew these tunnels and she would not question her direction.

"Just beyond the two lanterns ahead, lies a cross passage. To the left lives certain death or worse..." she paused, "and to the right is confusion if you do not know the underground. Just remain on course, no matter what. Aisha, promise me." The girl's grip tightened on Aisha's arm and she heard the urgency in her voice.

"I promise."

Chapter 16 – Pursuit of Destiny

Sultan's pace quickened as the Prince directed him back toward the stable. Cool water and sheltered cover was welcome in this heat and the horse sensed the change from his master's guidance. Sweat gleamed on the blue-black hide; flaring nostrils snorted dry dust into the air. The Prince sat affixed, rigid yet fluid, as if one with his regal mount. Sweat gleamed on his handsome tanned face, too, and he smiled knowing he was returning to one who would welcome his love given the kindness he extended during her capture. He rationalized his part in the plan as savior because he envisioned his aid to her as what one would extend in rescuing any helpless creature. She needed him for the wealth and comfort he could provide and he would cherish his role of protector during her inevitable rise to the Princess of Sarayi, in the palace of his father.

With Sultan content in the care of the stable boy, Haidar entered the quiet palace seeking cool liquid comfort of his own. First, raki for his parched throat; then he would look for the necessary company for his contained desires. He would extend his wishes beyond the congenial offerings given up to now. It was time to make his feelings known. The ride out into the palace lands helped to clear a muddied mind and made evident a destiny he thought to be the truth.

The filmy white liquid slid easily down his throat. Haidar pulled a sweat soaked tunic from his body and cooled himself with a water soaked cloth from the basin in his room. Standing in the alcove overlooking the canopies of the covered market place, he smiled as the sun dried the water on his skin, thinking of her touch; thinking of their bodies close together sweating, pulsing, and becoming one.

He hurried to redress, but as he pulled another tunic from a stack of freshly laundered linens, he stopped. His momentary silence only picked up the sound of air currents and the din of market noise. There was no movement in the house, which did not, at first, concern him. Often, all was quiet in his sequestered confines of the palace. He did not have the luxury of slave or many servants milling about as his father did in the main concourses of the palace. But even as the heat of day descended upon them, he found this to be the haunting silence of absence. He moved through the hallway, pulling the light shirt over his head and arms, calling out, as he ran.

"Saharra?" He peered into the room shared by the girls.

"Aisha?"

Fear overcame the confident Prince Haidar, as the reminder of counter abduction and revenge filled his thoughts. His evil brother vowed no rest until he was made to pay for the embarrassment caused in front of his harem the day he planned to rape Aisha in the alcove. That day, Prince Haidar rescued her from an uncertain future.

Loathing boiled in his stomach and he regretted not having killed his brother. The palace would be rid of a rodent worse than those who inhabit the underground tunnels. He stopped and looked toward the stone steps leading away from luxury to the bowels of corruption – *could he have taken them to the tunnels? He would never forgive himself if harm befell them at the hands of the rogues and his brother.*

The prince's hastened steps led him quickly to the lower levels and at the edge of grey shadow and the beginning of blackness, he stopped. There on the floor was evidence the girls were taken into the passageway below, and beyond. He stooped to pick up a soft leather hair tie.

Chapter 17 – Crossroads

As the tunnel wound its way deeper and deeper into the dark underground, swallowing the trio into the underbelly of the earth, a sudden rush of nerves washed over Aaslan. He found it hard to steady his breathing, caught up in the uncertainty of the next corner, the next beam of lantern light, and the indistinguishable sounds of the unknown beneath the land's surface. Their constant push forward with deliberate foot placement taxed his tired body and he realized fatigue and expectation could fool him into believing almost anything, at this point. It was highly probable it was his own blood pulsing through his ear drums, but he thought he heard the murmur of voices far, far off.

Udmurt's upraised hand signaled their halt – *he must have heard something, too*, Aaslan thought, as the seasoned tracker's actions confirmed his own suspicions. He knew the exhaled claim of his held breath would be too loud in the shadowed silence, so he hid his mouth in the crook of his elbow and felt the slow, moist warmth of air on his arm. There it was again, but it came to them more like echoed movements than discernible voices – *who would chance speaking in such a desolate place?* Discovery was inevitable.

Out of the range of the next sphere of light, Udmurt put a finger to his lips to quiet them and then motioned them on as they resumed their slow progression. A slight bend one hundred feet further in the passageway provided them a hidden vantage point, and allowed them time to decide their next move.

"We will wait here and watch that distant light fall – that is where the tunnel from the east meets with the north-south cross. It is not good to hasten our approach through that exposed area." Udmurt's voice was low and his words cautious. Their quiet interlude confirmed they were not alone on this underground journey. From the east, and from their very destination, came the recognizable sounds of movement. Though muted, the soft scraping of bodies passing close to the stone wall and firm padded footfalls on the hard surfaced floor carried on the air currents flowing in their direction.

"They do not sound intrusive," Izmir offered, in a low whisper.

"We will wait until they show themselves."

Udmurt was in no mood for surprises given their compromised surroundings; he slid low and crouched as a lion ready to pounce. Aaslan steadied himself with his back against the cool wall – the solid stone felt comforting in a strange way. Up ahead could be his demise or his destiny depending upon who countered their attempt to move east. In his mind, he could see his sister's sweet smile though her laughter was a distant memory. That day, her screams were the last he heard and they haunted him throughout his trip. *Now, so close* – Udmurt's hand reached back to touch his knee, alerting him to the image ahead.

There was brief movement, quickly retrieved and hidden again within the edge of the light at the tunnel crossroads. The approaching party exhibited cautions similar to their own and now there was no noise of movement. A covered head poked quickly into the realm of light surveying the north connecting passage. Like a turtle cautiously testing the outside world, it pulled in again to the shadows, only to poke out and check the south facing direction. For some time, eyes from deep within the folds of the hooded shelter pierced the darkness of the tunnel in their direction. The men did not move.

As they watched, two small figures stepped into the light and Udmurt's grasp tightened as a warning to Aaslan.

"Can we not move quicker?"

Aisha was careful to keep her voice low as she bent in close behind Saharra, placing her feet carefully and quietly as they moved step by step, touching her fingers to the wall to steady her motion. She felt the girl in front of her stop and she loosened the white knuckled grip on the back hem of the girl's tunic. Aisha stopped, too, aware she was putting them at risk by talking, even in the lowest of whispered tones, but she felt uneasy creeping slowly along a darkened underground passageway. Scurrying sounds from behind reminded her of rats – *she hated rats.*

"We must be cautious and I am sorry this is the only way out of here. I want you to be safe." Aisha felt the reassuring touch of Saharra's hand to her face. It was cool like the stone wall. The air currents created a soft breeze and she shivered; the scurrying sounds continued, increasing the shivers to a shudder.

"I hear something behind me."

"Just rats."

"I hate rats."

"Come. You go ahead, but go slow and stop inside that lantern light."

They continued, and with Saharra behind her, Aisha ignored the mysterious sounds of the tunnel. She imagined instead the sun on the earth above them, warming her throughout, bringing to her mind happy memories of home and her family – her brother. *Aaslan.*

She was so sure in her heart he would have saved her by now, but she was ever so thankful for the kindness of her companion and new friend. She smiled in the darkness as a sudden thought came to her, *how perfect Saharra would be for her brother – a beautiful couple.* The firm grasp of Saharra's hand on her shoulder, commanding her to stop, pulled her from her comforting thoughts.

"Shhh." The girls huddled close.

From behind them, there came more than just the sound of scurrying underground creatures. There came the definite sounds of footfall – steady and deliberate – someone was making their way toward them. Saharra grabbed Aisha's hand and they moved quickly down the centre of the passageway, their small feet landing softly upon the packed earth. As they neared the crossroads, Saharra stopped them and she listened intently for the sound of their follower.

Slowly, she poked a covered head into the light while viewing the north passage. There was no movement or sound coming from the home of the Road Rogues. She sought short refuge in the darkness and then peered out again, this time checking out the south extension of the tunnel. If they had to make a quick escape, she knew the hiding places there, but she hoped they would not need them. Her trained eyes pierced the darkness ahead of them. Their destined journey was within mere steps, albeit, dangerous ones. No sound or light or smell drifted her way as she held her gaze tempting fate to move and show itself.

Back within the shadows, she hugged Aisha and whispered a confirmation as resumption of their escape. She knew that on the other side of this junction lay freedom for her friend and sadness for her. She would lose someone she had grown to love and trust, if even only in a short time. She also knew punishment was inevitable and she might not survive.

"We are almost there, aziz."

He could hear movements far ahead in the tunnel and yet could not determine how many bodies moved and if the girls were carried or bound or kept from calling out in some other manner. He was certain his sister would know he would not rest until he found them. She was too precious to him despite all her claims of his unworthiness in the past. The young girl, Aisha, had become his most treasured desire and he knew how fond Saharra was of her, too. He could not let harm befall either one of them. He would stake his life on it – this time.

Prince Haidar hurried his pace knowing the tunnels by heart and by instinct. As a young boy, he grew up learning of escape and hard fought lessons. His brother made sure of that, often using him to prove prowess in front of his ragged, wretched friends. *Friends! Ha. Emir knew nothing of friendship* – Haidar thought, as he reminded himself of his brother's need to buy the devil and cater to his butchery. With the Road Rogues as his protective circle, no one would venture to counter an attack on the black prince while surrounded by murderers, kidnappers, and rapists.

The prince neared the last lantern light before the crossroads and stopped. He could see the silhouetted figures he pursued holding protectively to the side of the grey passageway. With the darkness enveloping the recesses of the tunnel, he was unsure of how many figures might still linger in the darkness. Even from his distant view, those out front seemed rather small in stature, but he could tell no more. They seemed to linger cautiously, evidence that they were experienced in the underground and cautious of exposing themselves at the tunnel's juncture.

He hurried his pace conscious of the sound on the pathway beneath his feet, wary of the scurrying of disturbed rodents and their incessant scratching. He needed to shorten the distance between them before they made a decision he would not be able to recover. As first witness to the exchange, the tunnel lanterns at the intersection cast a low light upon the meeting. Scurrying rats would forever more be silent, pushed from their own habitat by the merging of five bodies to that circle – the crossroads underground.

The men's rigid defence loosened upon glimpsing the young girls as they emerged from the shadows, the stealth of the mission now a thing of the past. But the girl's expressions revealed more than just the desperation of escape or the expectation of near freedom. There was also fear, as they continued to check behind them, unsure of where to run.

Aaslan was the first to react as he grabbed his sister's arms and pulled her gaze to his, his voice was lost to emotion as their eyes met. Aisha's fear turned to recognition and relief and she cried.

"I knew you would come."

He held her close, then, caressing her cheek and smoothing back the wild hair in what would be only a fleeting moment of reunion before the sound of another approaching brought the men to their warrior stance, the girls shielded behind their bodies, three abreast, readied.

"Stop. I command you – release them."

Prince Haidar strode into the light, brandishing a short blade from the sheath at the side of his leather waist belt. The white garments of his palace were smudged with tunnel dirt, his dark hair soaked with sweat.

"No, brother, please – we are safe." Saharra stepped from her place of protection behind Udmurt and Izmir, pleading with her brother yet knowing of her deception and its consequences.

"Saharra? Are you all right? Where is Aisha? Is she..."

Haidar did not finish his question as the blade was knocked from his hand by Aaslan who launched a flying leap at the prince, without thought to his own safety. The two landed hard in the dirt. Udmurt reacted, pulling Aaslan off the prince holding him back as the regal son lay coughing and sputtering from the sudden hit.

"Aaslan!"

Aisha moved in front of her brother interrupting the lion's gaze at his prey. She extended a hand to the prince despite the protests of her brother and his companions.

"Prince Haidar, this is my brother. I told you he would not rest until he found me." She was not afraid to claim the pride she felt for her brother even though it conflicted with her feelings for new found friends and quite possibly, love.

"He is a worthy opponent..." Prince Haidar replied, as he reluctantly released Aisha's hand; he stood and knocked the dust from his clothes, "...and an honorable brother." The prince showed the truth of his statement with a bow. "I am unsure at this moment how this is to end as I must claim what is rightfully mine – yet..." Haidar's gaze moved to sweep a loving look to Aisha, and he quickly continued, "I do not believe that to be of truth, despite my desires."

There was sadness in his voice as he realized the goodness in his heart could not be displaced by the expectations of his place in the Turkish society. His show of good faith was cut short by the increasing din of an approaching mass from the north; the sound of clashing metal met the group's ears – the smell of unwashed hide assaulted their airways.

"Who goes there!?" The demand came from depths of darkness.

"Come – we must go!" Saharra's voice was sharp with fear as she grabbed Aisha's hand pulling her toward the tunnel entrance to the south.

"No, my sister, not that way. Come, we will go back into the city through the palace entrance." His suggestion was met with obvious doubt in the hulking form of a Russian traveler. Udmurt stepped up to the prince, towering above in height and beyond him with size.

"You would have us trapped and executed." Udmurt's words were laced with hatred and he spat upon the ground beside the prince. "Your word is not worth anything to me, Prince." He gritted his teeth upon saying the word.

"By my word, I will die if harm comes to any of you. Please, we must make haste into the safety of the palace."

"Udmurt?" Aaslan was unsure of any more heroism, but he was not going to lose the sister he just found. His body was tired and his mind blank, yet it hurt with its fill of hateful questions.

"Boy, your life will not be worthy of a rat…"

"Please? My brother will keep his word – for me – he owes me his honor and will do right by his word." Saharra's voice pulled Udmurt from his stance and he gazed into rich brown eyes pleading with him to relent; his stolid demeanor wavered. Something in her voice soothed him beyond all explanation and he nodded despite an inner argument to hold his ground.

"We must go!"

Prince Haidar grabbed Saharra's hand and the group moved quickly out of the light into the shadows of the east tunnel. An uncommon camaraderie between royalty and commoner, Turkish elite and vagrant hunters, brothers and sisters, lion against lion – they made their way back into the grasp of the Mecca and all its palace powers.

Chapter 18 – At Mercy of the Palace

The warriors who followed were louder than they were swift.

The group who fled quietly back to the east, harbored a belief they had not been discovered. With the stealth of a lion pursuing its prey, the party followed Prince Haidar into the darkness and after a short time came upon the access to the palace. Upon his urging, they entered the hidden entryway, one that lay concealed just before they reached the passage leading out into the courtyard from beneath the palace and into the Mecca's covered bazaar.

Udmurt was certain earlier they would have taken that route for they could have easily merged into the crowds in the busy market place. He had ventured into that arena once before, long before this day, but without like success. Celebratory thoughts were cautious initial feelings as he was reluctant to claim victory in any form until they were safely on the road out of Istanbul. He saw the respect and devotion between brother and sister and it warmed the hunter's heart to know he was instrumental in uniting Aaslan and Aisha. They were long from calling this journey complete, however; the Road Rogues would not let them pass that easily had they come upon them. The choice to flee into the palace did not guarantee them their lives, let alone their freedom.

Udmurt was bothered by another emotion or, perhaps a feeling he better described as an undetermined sensation which he could not identify. It was upon looking into the eyes of the other girl, the sister to the prince, that he felt it the strongest. He could not shake the belief that he knew her soul through those eyes. They were the deepest, richest brown and he remembered only one other person with such soulful eyes – his own mother.

"Come, we linger too long here." Haidar waved them on with quick motions.

"They will follow – they are not that easy to deceive." Udmurt muttered low enough for the prince to hear him, but his words did not carry beyond to Aaslan and the girls. Izmir stood ground with his friend.

"My guards will keep any intruders at bay should they find the entrance, but we must not leave it to chance that we escape their wrath so easily."

"Why should I believe we will be safe in your keeping?"

"You must take my word at this point for it is all I can offer." The sincerity in the prince's voice hit Udmurt, and although cautious, he nodded in agreement.

"I will take your word, for it is all I have at this point, also."

There was an awkward moment of mutual silence between the three men cemented in the survival instincts they held sacred yet now placed in one another's hands. With a reassuring smile to Izmir, Udmurt urged his friend to follow their young companions up the stairs. Prince Haidar followed close behind.

Once inside the calm of the palace, Prince Haidar called to his servant who brought much needed refreshment for the group. He brushed the tunnel dirt from his clothes and smoothed his jet black hair with both hands while contemplating his next move. Aaslan's anticipated visit brought him much concern, but he could not fault a brother for seeking out the return of his sister. Over the course of the past few days, the scenario played itself over and over in his mind and still he could not formulate a satisfying solution. To fight for what he thought was his would be the way of his culture and the palace under the rules of his father's court. Still, watching their happiness in finding one another, he could not justify fighting for one he knew did not want to stay. He realized he must set her free to decide her own destiny. It would not be the way of his people, but it would be the way of his heart.

"We shall watch the entrance to the market place below to ensure the route of our pursuers."

The prince motioned to Udmurt and Izmir as he moved toward the balcony overlooking the city square below. It was mid day and the air was hot. Below, the open end of the covered bazaar was teeming with buyers and sellers and the colorful canopies shielded fresh products from the direct sun. The guards who watched the palace mingled with the crowds, sometimes resting up against the stone doors surrounding the busy square, at leisure but alert.

There was a commotion near the palace gate below the balcony and the men saw the hide draped warriors push their way through the people mingling in the entry way. Amongst the ragged men, strode Emir, his sharp, regal features striking against their bearded, leather-clad bodies.

Prince Haidar stepped back from view, with a cautious hand to Udmurt's arm.

"My own brother runs with nazar." It was a statement said without surprise.

"Will he bring them here?"

"He does not take refuge in my confines of the palace, but that does not mean he will stay away if he determines there is cause to enter."

"He is banished?"

"Not in my father's eyes, but in mine."

"We must not stay here." Udmurt glanced to Aaslan and Aisha, who he secretly considered his charges until such time they were delivered safely to their home. The responsibility was one he assumed when they chose to flee into the city instead of back to the confines of the forest.

"I must get them out of here before the Rogues discover they are here."

Haidar was slow to respond knowing that he would never see Aisha again if she were escorted back to her common home. They were of two worlds and their chance meeting placed within him a hope that he might find love. Now, it was falling away and he had but one choice to keep her.

Aaslan watched the hunters move from the balcony window to discuss what he assumed would be their next move. He had yet to let go of his sister's hand, afraid she might be taken again. He saw the prince gaze upon her as he spoke to his friends. He knew Aisha's move in the tunnel to protect the prince was one of fondness, for she would not have put herself into harm's way, for any other reason. He sensed there was a connection between them, but he could not identify how deep the feelings ran.

He then turned his attention to the prince's sister, Saharra, with growing interest. She had a rugged beauty disguised in royal garments. There was something about her, a charm he could not readily identify, yet it appealed to him in much the same way as when his travel companion first appeared. It was an immediate connection based on the situation, one that warranted a hesitant but needed trust.

"Aisha speaks highly of you."

Aaslan startled, thinking perhaps his words were not just in his head. He grew warm thinking of her hearing his thoughts, ones that took in her appearance and justified an admiration for her.

"Thank you. As I do of her."

"I wish we had met under different circumstances."

"There is always the future. Things can change."

"So, you are also naïve, like your sister." Saharra laughed softly, touching his arm as she watched his expression. Aaslan questioned the touch, silently, realizing it was culturally out of character for a Turkish woman to do so. He pulled his arm away.

"Not so naïve as to trust too quickly."

"I will have the stable prepare a cart for you." Haidar motioned to his servant who left with orders to prepare the wagon for the travelers.

"The young ones can hide under cover as we make our way to the forest road. We will take supplies with us." Udmurt felt the need to conceal from the prince that they had come prepared, their horses and supplies stashed just outside the city to the south. They intended to accomplish the mission and leave. It appeared to Udmurt that deception of the kind would be the safest way out under guise of a buying trip, the wagon loaded with supplies. He and Izmir would simply lead them safely out of town, unhindered.

"I will go with you."

Udmurt blinked with amazement at the prince. His statement was one of absurdity and impossibility. *How on earth did he expect them to just walk out of Istanbul unnoticed, if he rode along?*

"What?"

"I will go with you."

"And how do you propose we pass by the scrutiny of palace guards and warriors and commoners with regal escort in tow?"

"I am not your escort."

"What then?" Izmir growled. He could not take the frivolity of princely displays and was growing impatient with the whole exchange. He began to pace.

"I am leaving with you. I cannot keep what I want for mine so I must leave with you in order that I might have some chance in the future." His words were directed to Udmurt but his gaze rested upon Aisha. "I will not hold her as a prisoner to demand her affections."

Udmurt understood the complexity now of the task before them. It was not just simply a process of loading up and leaving without detection. The mission was now complicated with feelings and emotions that were difficult to keep hidden. He did not know what the outcome would be; he just knew they had lingered too long.

"We must leave, now."

The large man summoned the group together and he verbally laid the plan before them.

"Aaslan and Aisha you will ride inside the wagon. You must remain quiet and concealed from everyone. It is imperative that you follow instructions or we will not make it out from under the peering eyes of the city."

"Izmir and I," he paused, and continued when encouraged with a nod from Haidar, "and the prince, will walk as if travelers leaving with our wares." He noticed the look of alarm on Saharra's face and the surprised one shared by sister and brother.

"I shall go, too." Saharra was defiant in her claim. "You will not leave me alone to receive the ravages of the black prince."

"Saharra, of course, you will come, too." Aisha spoke up before any of the men had a chance to object. She would not allow her friend to remain behind.

Udmurt grunted his exasperation. *This was quickly turning bad.*

Chapter 19 – Palace Secret

"I will be quiet and remain covered," she spoke quickly as she dug into the bag she had packed for Aisha. "I am ready to go." She held close to her the woolen quilt rolled tightly and tied. Udmurt stared at her until she became uncomfortable and unsettled; she moved to stand beside the prince unsure of the traveler's sudden intense glare.

"Uf dah..." Udmurt grabbed the quilt from Saharra's hands, muttering under his breath the remainder of his exclamation. Tears formed in his eyes as recognition came to him and he looked to Saharra, questioningly. "Where did you get this?"

"What do you mean?" She pulled the colorful threaded quilt back and hugged it to her chest. "It is mine."

"It cannot be yours." The man's voice rose, yet he kept it low from discovery to any outside intruders. He wanted to yell but survival kept his emotions in check. "It belonged to my mother."

"That is not possible. My mother gave it to me."

"That is not the trappings of a Turkish princess, it is rough hewn and from handmade course." All were quiet and listened intently to the exchange. The prince did not speak up in defense of Saharra, but instead, remained equally as silent.

"It is mine and you cannot have it."

"I do not want to take it, but merely mean to identify how you came to possess it."

"My mother gave it to me."

"Then we would have the same mother."

The silence was punctuated with the exhale of held breath and exclamations of surprise and doubt. Aaslan put a hand to his friend's shoulder, holding him from further encounter yet encouraging an explanation.

"Udmurt?"

"There is a family crest on the corner – an oxen team against a rising sun."

Saharra did not have to look. She knew the quilt from corner to corner and often ran her finger over the very same emblem, wondering of its meaning. She knew there to be nothing so down to earth amongst the finery within the confines of the palace walls. She knew there had to be an explanation, but it was one that had eluded her and it was one her brother, the prince, failed to give her even when she grew more and more inquisitive. She refused to give up the belonging despite the prince's attempts to dispose of it. Now she knew why.

"Brother? Haidar?" She needed him to tell her despite the dilemma of the timing and situation. She needed him now to make things right. Tears formed in her eyes as her gaze met his, seeing and knowing his pain, yet still demanding the answers.

"You were taken from your home with your mother when you were young. The Road Rogues' legacy continues with similar deeds today. Your mother came to belong to the harem of my father and your fates were sealed forever here when she died. That quilt was the one possession my father saw no harm in you keeping, so he let you. My duty as a son was to raise you as my sister."

Udmurt's composure gave way as he fell to his knees at Saharra's feet. "They burned our home and killed my... our father." His voiced caught as he continued, "I was just a young boy, not even Aaslan's age. I have searched..." Overwrought, the hunter placed his face in his hands and shoulders heaved with silent sobs. After a short moment, he felt the soft touch of her hand to his head, much like the comforting gesture his mother once gave.

"You... are my brother?"

"Yes, Saharra, although I knew you as Inna..." Udmurt rose, regaining his composure and the hunter returned, ready to take charge. "We will have to deal with this later. We have to leave now. Prince, if you expect to travel with us, I suggest a change of clothing and recommend you follow my orders."

"I would expect to do no less."

The group made their way unnoticed through the quiet kafes' hallway and out toward the courtyard and the stables. There, awaiting their departure, was a team of draft ponies hitched to a loaded wagon with plenty of room for Aisha, Aaslan, and Saharra to hide amongst the barrels and woven sacks.

"We will go through the marketplace slowly as if perusing the stalls, while making our way to the south exit. Once out of the city, we will move into the forest cover and follow the shoreline of the sea until it is safe to travel by road." Udmurt looked around at the group, ensuring that everyone understood the escape route. "If we are separated for any reason, keep to that plan, and we will find each other in some way."

Confident everyone knew their place, Udmurt coaxed the team forward and the wagon set forth guided by three hide wrapped, leather bound hunters.

Chapter 20 – Beyond the Jeweled City

The dust and hot air choked them as they passed through street and stall, disguising their intended escape with contrived interest in the wares, with prolonged bartering that on one hand chanced discovery, and on the other, allowed them to blend into the expectations of travelers in the marketplace. Several times the prince, shielded behind the hunter's costume of hide and dirt smeared face, urged them forward beyond the prying eyes of watchful guards, pretending to show interest in a commodity stocked in the next market stall. If he could keep them moving, even slowly, they would make their way toward sure freedom.

What seemed like hours to the three stowaways hidden under sweltering hot layers in the back of the wagon, passed in a matter of fifteen minutes. Soon the din of constant conversation and barker's calls faded as the cart and the three men made their way out of the city. The wagon jostled as it took to the road, their journey on a southbound course. A bend in the road proved to be the relief Udmurt needed, but the emerging cover of trees was still just out of reach, a mile or so ahead.

"Keep still, my friends, eyes upon the way ahead. Wary of the hiding places to the ditches and the fields aloft." He talked slowly, without emotion as if in conversation to his friends who walked alongside the wagon. He did not want to give away anything too soon by assuming they were safe.

"We cannot breathe anymore under here." Aaslan's voice was low and it questioned their need to keep hidden.

"Just slow your thoughts and keep your heads down." Udmurt cautioned. "Just a little further and we can ditch the wagon for escape on foot into the trees." His eyes scanned the road ahead and followed the tree line that grew nearer and loomed larger as they walked.

"I do not see anyone following and no one appeared too interested in our movements while in the square. They should be safe." The prince spoke in similar movements and tones, copying Udmurt's lead. Izmir raised a hand to silence him, but Udmurt shook his head, signaling acceptance.

"At the forest edge we will help them out of the wagon and not before."

At Udmurt's signal they stopped and the hunters lounged against the wooden sides, scouring the nearby bay trees, long grass and shrubbery. The cover was welcome, but it could also hide dangers if they were not cautious in their approach.

After some time, when he was certain they were not being watched, Udmurt signaled to Izmir, who helped the young travelers one by one over the side of the wagon. They huddled against the wheel until all three were clear. Izmir then signaled back to Udmurt who stood with the prince, watching, pretending to shift the bags within reach at the end of the load.

As Udmurt waved his hand to the group huddled together, in a motion toward the trees, there was a loud wailing screech from the opposite side of the road, as Rogues covered in leafy branches, leapt from their hiding places amongst the weeds. It was as if vultures were waiting and now descended upon their prey.

"What the hell?"

Udmurt barely had time to mutter and prepare his defense as two large warriors rushed him and the prince, and knocked them both to the ground. The prince lay dazed while Udmurt came to his knees quickly, ready. Izmir was at his friend's side before the warriors had a chance to stand and together they met them head on. As they battled, another Rogue pulled the prince to his feet and, although he restrained him, the large man could not keep the prisoner from shouting a warning.

"Aaslan! Run!"

Without waiting for the hunters, Aaslan grabbed his sister and Saharra by the hands, pulling them with him as he ran for safe cover. Another hide cloaked warrior sprinted after the three as they made their way through the thick grass toward the trees. He was fit and moved quicker than the other Rogues and soon closed the gap between them. He grabbed Saharra's arm, pushing Aaslan to the ground when he tried to fight off the attacker. Aisha screamed as she struggled to help her friend, but was pushed to ground beside her brother.

"You will not escape me again." The hood covering the man's head and face fell backward revealing, Emir, the black prince.

"Let me go!" Saharra hissed, as she struggled with her captor.

Aaslan lunged at the prince, knocking him to the ground, but he was no match for the royal opponent and soon lay dazed in the grass, clutching his gut, winded and bruised. Aisha stayed next to him tending his wounds and from her vantage point watched as an angered Emir pulled Saharra back toward the wagon.

"Can you mangy beasts not do anything I ask?"

He threw the girl to the ground and moved toward the hunters, now subdued by the Rogue warriors. He saw Izmir who lay motionless, bleeding, face down in the road. Two of his men held Udmurt between them. He glanced up at the third easily restrained by a single Rogue and moved closer. Pulling away the leather cloak that hid most of the captive's face, Emir smiled.

"Brother. So you choose to disobey the laws of our land?"

"I choose to believe I am someone you are not."

"Aiding in the escape of slaves – that is sure, my Brother, to be penalized with death, despite who you choose to be or believe."

"Then bring death upon me, Brother, for I will not live under your rule."

Emir landed a solid blow into his brother's stomach and laughed as his twin doubled over, groaning in pain.

"You are not even worthy of living under my rule."

"Let them go, Emir, you have me."

"But I want it all, Haidar, unlike you I am not satisfied with half-done deeds."

Emir left his brother, ignoring further protests as if they fell upon deaf ears. He approached Udmurt who had taken the brunt of a beating once his friend was downed. It took a lot to restrain the big man, but when he finally just gave in he was bleeding profusely from the nose and mouth.

"Not so tough now."

Emir stood before him, taunting him by unsheathing and sheathing the long blade that hung at his side, smiling as if enjoying the task before him. "I have decided you will die, but at the very least I commend you, for you fought valiantly to save your friends. In your final moments, rest assured... I will take good care of the girls – not in the same manner as you, but they will be taken care of, no less. The young lion will die, too."

Udmurt lifted his head to stare directly into the face of the man who spoke so cavalier of life and death. Saying nothing, he managed to spit in Emir's direction.

Emir drew and raised the blade and Udmurt counted his final moments, unable to fight. He was then surprised to watch the prince's expression change from smug victory to agonized surprise. Emir fell forward dropping the blade by his side, a dagger driven deep into the back of his neck. Saharra stood before Udmurt, her hands quivering. The shocked men holding Udmurt let him go and he fell forward to his knees, quickly steadied by his sister.

The Rogues, as if uncertain and confused by the death of their leader, turned to Prince Haidar. The bruised royal stood free from the restraints of their fellow warrior who now lay at his feet, a long blade skewered through his back. Aaslan stood triumphantly beside Haidar, pleased the experience of taking down a charging boar stayed fresh in his mind. The brave lion rejoiced.

The group was silent as they buried Izmir not far from where he fell that day. Under the overhanging boughs of a bay laurel tree, he was laid in peace with a crude stone marker to signify his life on earth. Udmurt bowed his head and the hunter was silent for a long while before he murmured some words Aaslan did not recognize. When he turned to face them, the sorrow for the loss of his friend showed briefly, and then it vanished as his focus returned to the journey that still lay ahead.

Udmurt helped Haidar load the body of his brother into the wagon. He knew the prince suffered even though Emir would have killed him first if he had been given the chance. He knew he was spared only to witness the killing of those who might protect the innocent. Haidar would most likely face his punishment once he returned to the palace and his father's rule. Without a brother to contend his rights, Haidar would be an only son and might, if he survived, retain the rights given to such a position when the time came.

"Are you sure you want to go back?" Udmurt could not believe that honor would run as deep as foolishness. They loaded the body of the dead warrior into the wagon alongside his brother's.

"I must face my father and take what he deems to be my fate."

"Perhaps, it will not be all bad?"

"Perhaps, you do not know my father." Haidar tried to displace Udmurt's concern with a slight laugh and slowly put a hand to the large man's shoulder.

"There is no honor in revenge," Udmurt surmised.

"There is no honor in deceit."

"What do you want to do with these?" Udmurt motioned to the Rogues who were made to kneel under threat of similar death. They appeared too full of fear to move, but Aaslan stood by with the blade, readied to comply.

"Bind their hands – I will take them to my father."

"A peace offering?" Udmurt laughed and ripped a strap of leather into strips, binding their hands and tying them to the side rails of the wagon. "Let 'em walk."

Aaslan, his duty complete, approached the prince. He felt he had to say his piece before the prince left them to their journey home.

"Prince Haidar?"

"Brave Aaslan, how can I repay you?"

"Repay me?" Aaslan was surprised. "There is no need, for I owe you my gratitude in protecting and watching out for my sister. True, you should have set her free, but it is because of your kindness that she lives and I am truly thankful for that."

The prince was touched by Aaslan's words and knew him to be more of a brother than he could ever be. He stopped as the realization hit him – *he would no longer fill that role, in any respect.* His own brother was now dead, and the sister he grew to love as if she were truly related, would be leaving.

"Take good care of both of them."

Aisha was upset when she discovered the prince would not be traveling any further with them. She understood his need to return home for she, too, longed for that comfort. She let her naivety block out the depth of his calling so she would not imagine the need for him to answer to his father for his transgressions. The one thing she knew for sure was that she had grown fond of him.

"Aisha, I will look for you in the future. I feel we were meant to be together and I have a deep sadness in my heart letting you go, but I know I must. It is only right. If our paths are meant to cross, they will do so again." He had pulled her close and kissed the top of her head in a loving gesture that made her feel safe and sorry all at once. She let herself believe in his words for they were comfort. She also let him go, believing in his promise.

"This will solidify my promise to you Aisha, my future Princess of Sarayi." He handed her a silver box, a lion carved upon the lid, lying in the shade of a bay tree. "Open it later. Remember my words. Remember me."

She watched as he made ready to return home.

Chapter 21 – Out of the Forest

The party of four moved through the woods without further incident and with little conversation. For some time, they pursued the final leg of their journey home in silence. It had been an emotional parting and tearful for everyone, even hunter and brave lion, if all were to admit honestly to the effects of the recent outcome of events. Half of the party came to know only briefly the man Prince Haidar proved to be, but the women claimed a closer connection having shared heart and hearth.

Aisha accepted her good-bye promises from the prince and was able to come to terms with leaving him behind having viewed the gift he bestowed upon her at their parting. During their first night camp, under cover of treed canopy, while snuggled securely between protective brothers, she secretly admired the shimmering gold lion broach that lay nestled in silk wrap, its ruby eyes bright and hopeful.

Saharra, however, wrestled with betrayal and confusion, yet felt sadness in leaving the brother she once knew. This upset her. Although conflicted, she knew she would come to accept the happiness in finding the true brother she was stolen from long ago. She had no recollection of the night described by Udmurt in his tearful confession. The years since, were filled with bittersweet childhood memories of life within the palace as a Turkish princess. As a young girl growing up, she was without want for material goods, yet lacked emotional ties to anyone but Prince Haidar. He was her only companion once her mother's health failed and she looked to him for protection. When he failed to defend her from the ravages of his violent brother, she had to forgive him for she had nowhere else to turn. To engage his ongoing promise of protection, she pledged domestic servitude to him and chanced a safe and happy life, albeit, without personal destiny.

It was with uncertainly she realized during their second night of freedom, there were no dreams attached to her imaginings, for the pledge she made to Haidar was the only future she ever expected. Now, lying there alone with her thoughts, safely surrounded by others who shared a life that would have normally been hers, there was also fear. *What was to become of me? How will I adjust to life outside the palace?*

Her thoughts came to rest on Aisha's brother, Aaslan, partway through the third day. She watched him as he forged ahead through the trees, never complaining or demanding. *Had he always been so honored to prove his love to a sister? Would he prove his love to another in the same way?* Saharra felt her face flush with self-inflicted embarrassment. No one knew her thoughts yet she felt as though she just screamed them at the top of her lungs. *Aaslan, would you ever love someone like me?* She lowered her eyes and continued walking, contemplating her options.

She chanced another look to him as they continued their journey through the undergrowth just off the open road. *Could there be a chance for me with someone like him?* As she pondered the question, he looked back upon the party following at close range. He looked directly at her and he smiled. It was then she knew there might be hope.

As they trudged wearily along the dusty road, familiarity hit Aaslan and Aisha at almost the same moment. It was without obvious change in the forest pattern or reason evident to Udmurt. The hunter was familiar with the road but he knew they were familiar with the surroundings. He could feel the pair's excitement mount as they passed a creek bed meandering to the left through the thick trees cutting a small water filled path in the undergrowth. The road was carved through nature's trails and met at this juncture with the stream, close and inviting to thirsty travelers.

Aisha stooped to cup a refreshing mouthful to her lips, encouraging Saharra to do the same. Both girls then mopped their dusty faces with the hem of their water soaked tunics. As Aisha stood, the shrill of a forest bird frightened her and she crouched again, head in hands, sobbing.

"Aisha! It is only a bird."

Aaslan comforted his sister knowing that the memory of that first day of their journey still haunted her despite all the circumstances in between. Udmurt stooped to splash water on his weathered face then pulled the girl to her feet meeting Aaslan's concerned eye. A quick shift of his eyes to the trees signaled a warning to his young friend.

"'Tis only a bird, young one. Let us be going now – you are almost home."

The girl was convinced but Udmurt was not, and as the party made their way down the road, he remained alert to the noises of the forest. A crest in the road gave him discomfort when he could not see past the slight rise and was panicked when Aaslan and Aisha began to run. His relief only came when he saw the small settlement of wood shingled cabins ahead in a clearing.

He felt the small hand of his sister slip into his as their companions left them to follow at their leisure. His heart beat faster knowing he would soon finish the task he took upon himself to complete. He glanced down at Saharra walking trustingly by his side and realized he now had a new responsibility. This concerned him, but was of inconsequence at that moment. In front of him was the reason he put so much into his duty, his responsibilities, and his never ending search.

"Mama! Pappas!"

An astonished look of relief and doubt and long trusted prayers crossed the farm woman's face, as she stood for a moment, dumbfounded by the appearance of her daughter and son. Disbelief turned to tear filled emotion, as she dropped the trowel she held poised over the garden row. She pulled her skirts high as she ran toward the pair, tears turned to crazed laughter as she called to her husband who appeared at the corner of the stable, hay bundle in arm. He, too, joined his wife and soon all four were embraced in a family hug.

"Oh, my babes are safe!"

"We thought you were..." Their father could not finish what he dared not think the whole time they were missing. "Your uncle did not know what happened to you. We were ill with worry and dread. Oh, my. Oh, my." He grabbed each child and clasped their face tight giving a quick kiss to each cheek. Then, suddenly, he was aware of the others who were present.

"You brought my babes home?"

Whether it was maturity or the trappings of a traveler and a hunter that gave away a brother's journey to their home, Udmurt did not care. The happiness with which Aaslan and Aisha were received, reminded him of what life was all about. He draped a loving arm over his sister's shoulder and she smiled up to him. It was at that moment he knew they could find a place together in a common world.

"We both did."

He spoke proudly, claiming responsibility while sharing the glory.

Journey of Brothers - Glossary of Terms

Aaslan = "lion" in Turkish

Aisha = "alive and well" in Arabic

Aziz = "beloved" in Arabic

Emir = "charming prince" in Arabic

Haidar = "lion" in Arabic

Hazine = "treasures" in Turkish

Inna = "strong water" in Russian

Izmir = city in Turkey

Kafes = confines for successors to the throne

Nazar = using the word here to refer to evil. In Turkey = "evil eye" and nazar or evil stones are used to ward off the effects of the evil eye.

Pastirma (basṭurmā) = A cured and dried meat originally from Turkey or Armenia usually made from beef fillet. Sun-dried slices of meat are coated with a paste made of garlic, fenugreek seeds, paprika, and salt and left to cure. It is usually eaten for breakfast with fried eggs or, in Egypt, with the stewed bean dish known as fūl.

Pizdets na khui blyad = Russian roughly translates to "F--- it all. F------- load of bull----!"

Saharra = "desert" of Arabic origin

Sessiz = "quiet, silence" in Turkish

Silniy = "strong" in Russian

Udmurt = a people and an area of Russia or Origin: < Russian udmúrt < Udmurt: a self-designation (ud- (compare Votyak) + murt man, human being). Dictionary.com Unabridged

Uf dah = of Norwegian origin; an exclamation of surprise, dismay, exhaustion, relief as a result of sensory overload and can even be used in place of swear words.

About the author:

Born and raised in Edmonton and Sherwood Park AB, Linda found a place to feel right at home with her writing passion - the Writers Circle and the Writers Foundation of Strathcona County are important components of her writing life. Although poetry is her first love and was the mainstay of her writing for many years, screenplays, novels, short stories, non-fiction articles, and blogs have made their way into her writing repertoire.

For this author, dedication to the craft involves a constant learning – sharing – creating cycle:

- always **learn** new things to improve your skills

- **share** time and expertise with others to promote their work and achievements
- actively **create** your own new work

The balance shifts from one to another, but the triad is always there in one way or another. With focus and forward momentum, fulfillment of a writer's dream is only a process away.

One key piece of advice this author offers and lives:

> *"Be true to your creative spirit."*

Her mantra:

> *"Learn the rules like a pro, so you can break them like an artist."*
>
> ~ Pablo Picasso

… break all the rules... and be your own artist.

Linda is a published author with ebooks available on Smashwords and Amazon Kindle. She has written several electrical industry papers for her job as Business Management Coordinator with the AFREA in Sherwood Park. She is a contributing writer for the online news magazine Strathcona Connect. To read blog posts inspired by her writing life and to link with fellow writers, visit Linda's blog:

http://www.wildhorse33.wordpress.com

Follow her on Facebook and @wildhorse33 on Twitter

Made in the USA
Charleston, SC
25 April 2014